'I don't believe in conscience. I don't believe
in God. And I certainly don't believe in
politics. Family? Hah! What's family?
And as for love – love is the biggest lie of all.
I believe in one thing. *Me!*'

Neil Arksey lives in Bloomsbury, but spends much of his time in a fantasy world. As well as writing novels for young people, he works as a scriptwriter and story consultant. He has storylined several popular TV soaps and dramas, in the UK and abroad. When he's not writing he is often to be found swimming in an outdoor pool in the heart of London.

www.neilarksey.co.uk

Books by Neil Arksey

AS GOOD AS DEAD IN DOWNTOWN
MACB
PLAYING ON THE EDGE
RESULT!

NEIL ARKSEY

AS GOOD AS DEAD IN DOWNTOWN

PUFFIN

PUFFIN BOOKS

Published by the Penguin Group
Penguin Books Ltd, 80 Strand, London WC2R 0RL, England
Penguin Group (USA), Inc., 375 Hudson Street, New York, New York 10014, USA
Penguin Books Australia Ltd, 250 Camberwell Road, Camberwell, Victoria 3124, Australia
Penguin Books Canada Ltd, 10 Alcorn Avenue, Toronto, Ontario, Canada M4V 3B2
Penguin Books India (P) Ltd, 11 Community Centre, Panchsheel Park, New Delhi – 110 017, India
Penguin Books (NZ) Ltd, Cnr Rosedale and Airborne Roads, Albany, Auckland, New Zealand
Penguin Books (South Africa) (Pty) Ltd, 24 Sturdee Avenue, Rosebank 2196, South Africa

Penguin Books Ltd, Registered Offices: 80 Strand, London WC2R 0RL, England

www.penguin.com

First published 2004
1

Text copyright © Neil Arksey, 2004
All rights reserved

The moral right of the author has been asserted

Set in Monotype Sabon
Typeset by Rowland Phototypesetting Ltd, Bury St Edmunds, Suffolk
Made and printed in England by Clays Ltd, St Ives plc

British Library Cataloguing in Publication Data
A CIP catalogue record for this book is available from the British Library

ISBN 0-141-31052-9

Seni canımdan çok seviyorum

Thanks
To my mum and the Royal Literary Fund, without
whose support this book could not have been
completed.

Sounds that travel far and wide,
stormy weather doth betide.

                                    Portobellan proverb

Contents

1

Earth, Water, Wind and Fire

An osprey climbs the sky.

Warmed by the blazing sun, upward spiralling currents of air lift her. Her muscular wings beat tirelessly on, carrying her higher.

Temperature falls by degree. The atmosphere grows thinner. But still she presses on. Climbing.

Seven miles up. Through sheer determination she has breached the lower limits of the stratosphere. And, looking down now with dark glittering eye, what does she see?

A wide disc.

Little brown portions on a big blue-green plate, decorated with wisps of white.

And beyond. The deepest blackness of empty space.

She sees the world in all its roundness.

The Earth.

And having flown higher than any osprey ever, she glides, taking it all in. Savouring the moment.

Then, with the tiniest tilt of head, and the smallest adjustment to the alignment of wing, the osprey begins her descent.

As the air thickens and temperature begins to rise, she hears its quiet roar.

Her descent is gradual, effortless; finding and following currents. Down there, far, far below, a faltering line traces where land meets sea. With time, the line will shift. And future ospreys will follow.

Down, down, down she glides and lower still, till past the very highest wisps of cloud, she spots what she's looking for – a point, a blip in the line. From this height it's still the merest speck, but growing. She cleaves towards it, dropping more quickly now.

The blip becomes a spot, becomes a patch, becomes larger and larger. A labyrinth unravelling. Intersecting lines, grids, patterns, streets, buildings, boroughs . . .

A coastal metropolis, old buildings and new. Not one city but two. Two cities sliced apart by a livid scar. Two cities divided by history, hatred and ugly fortifications. Gleaming Nebula – capital of a vast nation bearing the same name. And crumbling city state Portobello – trapped against the shore by the sprawling bulk of its neighbour.

And now the osprey swoops, down over Nebula's sleek towers, bastions of wealth and power, soaring and shimmering on the high ground. Down over pretty, poor Portobello, with its ramshackle houses and tenements, its medinas and temples crowded together on the gentler slopes. And its harbour, like an azure pincushion, bristling with masts.

On, over the long white beach the osprey glides, on towards the peninsula's narrowed headland, a finger pointing the way south to migrating flocks.

Sweeping low she gathers speed, skimming the tiny coves scattered amongst the rocks. A sheer granite wall thrusts defiant against the ocean swell. Accelerating, on a collision course with its highest outcrop, she arcs into a steep climb boosted by invisible uplift, and roars vertically up, up, up the cliff face, exploding like a bolt into the blue . . .

2

Shock and Fury

'Waah-ha-heey!'

Kai, the tangle-haired boy on the flat roof, laughed and whooped with delight as the distant osprey banked into the sun. Shaded by his hand, his keen, startling green eyes had watched the bird's graceful swoop across the city, its low glide out over the beach to the headland, and breathtaking stunt-filled vertical climb. Now twisting, the bird levelled out for another pass over the perfect sea and back inland.

'Did you see that, Clod?'

'Wh-wh-what?' The boy at his feet lay prone, peering nervously over the edge, down into the street below.

'Magnificent!'

'Wh-wh-what? I don't see it.'

'Not on the ground. Look! Up there. Look at it!' Kai pointed. 'Here it comes again! Isn't it the most beautiful, amazing thing?'

With a strenuous grunt, Clod twisted his neck around, shielded his eyes and peered.

'When I was still a sprat,' said Kai, 'my ma used to take me to the beach. I was a natural in the sea.'

'You w-w-won't catch me anywhere n-n-near it.'

Kai chuckled. 'I remember once swimming underwater with a shoal of sardines. I flipped on to my back, looked up through the shimmering surface and saw this enormous bird dropping from the sky . . .'

'Wh-what happened?'

Kai followed the soaring bird with his eyes. It was directly overhead. He pointed again. 'You see it now?'

Squinting against the sun, Clod nodded.

'The bird was the same as that. An osprey. Their wing-spans are wider than you are tall. Imagine!' He stretched his arms out in front of him, curling his fingers like claws. 'As it hit the water, talons outstretched to snatch a fish, I *grabbed it*!'

'You d-d-did *what*?'

'Grabbed it! Grasped it round its legs.' Kai laughed. 'You should have seen the fury in its eyes. As it beat its wings it actually raised me out of the water!'

Clod's eyes widened. 'Th-then what?'

Kai was enjoying the tale. 'It screeched. It flapped its wings. And then it stabbed me very hard with its beak, till I let go! Here . . .' He held out his hand. 'See the knuckles? Got the scars to prove it.'

In the sky above them, the osprey was circling on a thermal that carried it in over the city.

'They return every year to nest,' said Kai. 'Out on the headland.' He watched the osprey as it headed over the sea. It was calling. He cupped his hand to his ear. *What was it saying?*

'Kai . . .' There was wariness in Clod's tone. 'I hate to bring you b-b-back to earth but . . .'

'There's a job to be done?'

Clod nodded.

'Well – aren't you supposed to be watching the street?'

'But you s-s-said . . .' Clod spluttered.

'. . . to watch the bird?' Kai grinned. 'OK. Come on

then.' He gestured towards the street. 'Take a look. See if you can spot our man yet.'

With all the grace of an overturned beetle trying to right itself, Clod rolled himself over and resumed his earlier position. He peered down into the street, his nose pressed against the raised edge of the roof. 'Oh my G-G-God! He's there!' There was a touch of panic in his voice. 'Quick, Kai! It's h-h-him!'

Kai stepped up on to the low parapet. Noise from the bustling crowd five storeys below assaulted his ears. The street was one of several that fed into the main market square. One of several where contraband was traded. Familiar territory. 'So which one is he?' he called to Clod. 'How's he dressed?'

'You c-c-can't miss him,' said Clod. 'He's the largest m-m-man in the street.'

'I see him,' said Kai. 'Shiny bald head. And a posse of maybe fifteen men around him?'

Clod nodded.

'Distinctive. I've seen him before. A few times. Always wondered who he was. Looks a nasty piece of work.'

'And is.'

'Right.' Kai pulled the hood of his jalabi down low on his forehead, so his eyes were in shadow. He winked at Clod. 'All set?'

Clod nodded.

'See you on the other side!'

The building, like most in the area, was a tenement: separate apartments on each floor, with a shared staircase and hallway. On his way down, Kai ran through his checklist and plan of action. He had all the equipment he needed. His exits were prepared. He knew what he was going to do.

In the shadows of the front porch, he paused and reached

5

down. Earlier he had sharpened a steel spoke and concealed it inside the seam of his boot. Now, as he slid the tool up his sleeve, he checked its point against his thumb. Like a needle. *But would it be long enough?*

In the street, the Big Man and his entourage drew close. Dressed in leather and furs, the Big Man's fat wrists and neck were draped in thick chains of gold. His girth was enormous. His voice matched his demeanour, loud, haughty and dripping with self-importance. A sour ugliness characterized his face – mean eyes lost in greedy flesh, a scowl as permanent as a scar, and a thin, sneering mouth concealed behind a beard.

Kai watched. This beast had amassed a fortune kidnapping children, murdering them and selling their organs across the border in Nebula. And yet the militia, the city's police force, gave him round-the-clock protection. Sickening! Portobello was not just a lawless city but a heartless one too. All that was about to change.

Moving out from the doorway and down the steps, Kai slipped into the crowd. Slim and still some way from being fully grown, it was easy for him to squeeze through the tightly packed bodies to the middle of the street. Here two streams of shoppers rubbed shoulders as they shuffled in opposite directions. It was warm, and sour odours of stale sweat mingled with the pungent spices of market stall food. Edging his way across, Kai joined the flow of people on the furthest side.

As soon as he was in position, the approaching phalanx of militiamen came into view. Assault rifles at their hips, they strode with swagger, shoving people roughly out of their way as the group moved slowly forwards. Head bowed, but watching keenly, Kai waited. *Timing would be everything.*

The Big Man paused to point at something, his arrogant laughter rolling above the sound of the crowd. The armed guard halted too and turned to share the joke. Frustrated by this temporary obstruction, the restless crowd behind muttered in discontent and tried to push past. Militiamen glowered and shoved them back.

Kai watched as an argument between two guards and a woman developed into a tussle. *This is the moment.* Slipping between the two guards he dropped through the legs of a third and scrambled to his feet on the other side. The spike was ready in his palm. The Big Man towered above him, more than twice his height and several times his girth, scowling at this breach of his security.

Kai stepped forwards, looking for signs of concealed body armour. He needed to be swift. He hadn't planned this but, '*Dadda!*' he yelled. The more confusion he could create the better.

Puzzlement flitted across the Big Man's face. It darkened. The piggy eyes glared.

With a short run and a leap, Kai scrambled up the mass of fur and leather and grabbed hold of the gold neck chain. He dug in with his knees. '*Dadda!*' he cried again and jabbing the spike at the chosen spot, he pressed himself against the Big Man's chest in feigned embrace. Beneath his palm the sharpened point plunged through garment, flesh and muscle. Pushing with all his weight, Kai felt it grate against rib. The Big Man's hands clutched, but Kai pressed on till it was all the way home. *In to the hilt.*

He dropped to the ground.

A startled look spread across the monstrous features. The Big Man staggered, his guards and the crowd gasped. His arms flailed, his knees buckled and, with a rasping drawn-out grunt, he keeled forward into the gutter.

Stunned, militiamen and the hushed throng around them stared at the enormous body sprawled lifeless on the cobbles.

Kai had already slipped into the crowd. Disappeared.

3

Pain

Another howl swelled, filling the room till it stretched reed thin, wavered and collapsed in a tumble of sobs.

Kai lay in the dirt, curled against the wall, his knees pulled tight into his chest. Rocking himself back and forth like a baby. *What was happening?*

'This is t-t-terrible!' Clod crouched beside him, frantic. 'I d-d-don't understand . . . You're not in-in-injured?'

Kai shook his head and screwed his eyes shut. His breaths came in gasps, and long shuddering sighs. *Was it passing?* He clutched himself tighter. *Hold it. Press it – whatever it was – down.*

'The j-j-job itself seemed to go s-s-so well,' Clod's voice quivered.

Clod had never seen him like this. Nobody had. This wasn't him. He was Rock and Fire. He didn't do this – didn't do weakness . . . feelings . . . falling apart . . .

Clod hobbled to the window. 'There's st-st-still n-no sign of any mil-l-litia in the street.'

Lucky he'd made it here. The abandoned apartment had been the right choice for hiding.

'I d-d-didn't see what happened after. I heard sh-sh-shooting. Was it . . .' Clod cleared his throat, '. . . gruesome?'

Kai shook his head.

'I want to help,' said Clod. 'Tell me wh-wh-what to do . . .' He touched Kai's shoulder.

Kai flinched. The hand was withdrawn. He was trembling. *Deep breath*. 'Did you hear anything?' His voice was faint, fragile-sounding. Like a frightened child.

'How d'you m-m-mean?' Clod was baffled.

Kai bit his lip. *Clod hadn't heard it. He would have known what he meant*. The painful ache welled up again – like someone had punched a hole through his gut. His strength, nerve, confidence – all sucked out and drained away.

'I was on th-th-this side,' said Clod, 'when the g-gunfire started. It sounded like b-b-bedlam.' He waited for a response. 'P-people must have been hit . . . ?'

Kai nodded. 'Must have.' *Push whatever it is back. Focus on events*. Another deep breath. 'The street was jammed with people. And those brainless militia pigs just started blasting.' *That felt better*.

He had been fine right after the deed. Rock and Fire. Heart of Ice. Making his exit, another job successfully completed. 'One of them finally yelled at the citizens to get down. But by then I was almost across the street.' He had been cruising. On a wave. 'Couple of shots hit the plaster as I ducked inside the building.'

This was good. Focusing on what happened was helping. He felt stronger. He opened his eyes. 'That's as close as they got.'

Clod gave him a gentle, good-to-see-you smile. 'So th-th-then what happened?'

Kai rolled over to face him. 'I raced up the stairs, on to the roof . . .' *Everything had still been fine*, '. . . dashed over the plank to this block and pulled it across so no one could follow . . .'

'Th-th-thereby vanishing into th-th-thin air!' Clod's smile strengthened. 'All according to p-p-plan.'

Kai nodded.

The gut-wrenching feeling again. Another shuddering sigh. 'But when I was on the stairs here, on my way down ...' *That had been when it started. That was when ...*

Clod waited.

'I heard something, Clod.' *Rock had crumbled, ice melted, dissolved ...*

'Wh-wh-what?' Clod frowned, puzzled. 'What did you hear?'

'I'm not sure.' His voice was barely audible, a feeble croak. 'A terrible sound.' He was trembling again, shaking. *He had heard it before. A long time ago ...*

'Oh my God!'

'What!?'

'I know! I know what it was – the sound.'

'What!' Clod leant close. 'Wh-wh-what, Kai? What?'

Kai felt tears. He closed his eyes. 'Death.'

4

Escape

A red light had been flashing over the library exit for the best part of an hour. It indicated a security alert. The library staff had locked the group of them in and left. Something that had never happened before. From outside in the corridor the muted wail of a siren could still be heard.

'Every sixty seconds, somewhere in the world a child less fortunate than us drops dead from starvation.'

'I don't care!' snapped Phoebe, exasperated.

A self-satisfied smile stretched across Aristotle's face. He had managed to turn the situation into an intellectual discussion. And now he was winning the argument and he knew it.

'As long as we are locked up in here,' said Phoebe, 'we can't ever actually know that. Or anything else about the world for that matter.'

'It's a fact.'

'Exactly!' said Phoebe. 'To us, in here, that's all it can ever be. One of an infinite number of facts. What does it have to do with our lives? We're not part of the real world.'

Aristotle shrugged and gestured. The broad sweep of his hand said look around you. 'Ours is not such a bad life.'

'We're prisoners!' Phoebe gestured angrily towards the mirror, one of the disguised windows, through which they could be discreetly monitored twenty-four hours a day. There was one in every communal area. 'We have been since we came into this world. We're objects – guinea pigs – probed, tested and examined every waking and sleeping moment.'

'There are worse ways to live.'

That essentially was Aristotle's argument: why, when they had such comfortable lives, risk everything for the sake of freedom?

A growling noise issued from Phoebe's throat. 'You just don't get it, do you?'

'Come on, sis.' Phoenix tugged at her elbow. 'I told you. You're wasting your time.' He pulled her away.

'This could have been our chance!' yelled Phoebe, shaking free of her brother. 'If we had acted together while the staff were busy dealing with this crisis, we might have done something...' She jabbed an accusatory finger towards Aristotle and the group gathered behind him. 'But you're gutless! All of you – *totally*!'

'Cautious,' said Aristotle. 'And realistic. That's what I'd call it. Better that than dead. And dissected.'

Phoebe snorted. She knew what he was alluding to. There were rumours of other attempts at escape. 'We've all heard those stories. But who starts them, did you think of that? You really believe they'd shoot children. Shoot to *kill*?'

Faces said they did.

'Think about it,' said Phoebe, 'each and every one of us represents decades of research and development, unimaginable financial investment. Why destroy that with a bullet?'

'Fear,' said Aristotle. 'In here, under tight control, we are Nebula's evolutionary advantage. We are their future:

13

intellectually and physiologically superior, better adapted for a changing environment. But once we cross that line, once we're out there . . .' He shook his head. 'The situation is turned upside down.'

'We can pass on our genes,' said Phoenix.

'Exactly,' said Aristotle.

Phoenix grinned, mischief glinting in his eye. 'We will become their worst nightmare.'

'*You* think about it.' Aristotle's fierce gaze was directed at Phoebe. 'To prevent that, they will do *whatever it takes*.'

Phoebe lay awake in her bed. The night was warm and her mind was racing. If she was ever going to escape, it would just be with Phoenix. She knew that for certain now. From the start he had tried to persuade her they should work together in secret and not involve the others. This evening's rebuttal showed he had been right all along.

They had been planning their escape for over a year but still hadn't set a date. A lot of it they had worked out down to the smallest detail. But there were still some problems to be solved. Like how to get past the twenty-four-hour guards at the entrance to their block. And what to do if their plan succeeded and they got out. *What then?*

Phoebe sighed, stretched and threw back the covers. This was shaping up to be another restless night. Phoenix, she knew, was so eager to leave. He didn't show it the same way as she did, but she could read the signs. Whenever she brought up getting past the guard on the entrance, he tapped his nose and told her he had a way.

Would there ever be another chance like today? And would they be more ready if there was? It had been the younger kids on the other side of the compound who had created the diversion, causing all the problems. Tearing up the place, screaming and shouting in a riot of fear, scared out of their wits by the eerie new sounds. The noises from the ground.

The noises had occurred before, several times, but always so briefly and so faintly that everyone, even if they noticed, soon forgot them. But today's episode had been strong and sustained – impossible to ignore. No wonder the little ones had been terrified. It had really been scary.

And all the unmodifieds – the staff, the guards and everyone else – they couldn't hear it. So how could they reassure the little ones or explain what was causing it? None of them had any idea why the youngsters were going crazy. It had been all hands on deck. Even the librarians had been summoned to help.

Had the guards been called away too? Unlikely. Security were much too cautious for that.

What was that? Phoebe sat up with a start. Her bedside light was still on, the covers were on the floor. She must have fallen asleep after all. A sudden sound made her jump. What was it? Someone knocking. At this hour, it could only be one person. She slid from the bed and hurried to open the door.

'Phoenix!' He was dressed in outdoor clothes. Strapped to his waist was the small pack. She knew what this meant. She had an identical one. They had prepared them together, in secret.

'Time to go!' he whispered, pushing past her into the room.

Phoebe closed the door behind him. 'I don't understand! What's going on?'

'Didn't you hear it?'

'Hear what?'

15

'There was another episode – the noise from the ground. Quite a long one. It must be causing bedlam amongst the little ones. All the night staff are over there.'

'But there are no sirens.'

'Perhaps they didn't want to wake us.' There was a wild look in his eyes. Urgency. Excitement. 'The guard has gone too!'

'How do you know?'

'I've been to check.'

Phoebe was still feeling drowsy. 'And you're sure?'

'Yes.' Phoenix's grin caught the light. 'This is it! The moment we've been waiting for!' He guided her gently but firmly towards the chest of drawers. 'Come on, sis. Get dressed. We don't have much time.'

Pushing through the narrow gap, Phoebe felt the air's dampness on her skin. In one deft movement she sprang up and on to the roof. She was fully alert now, no doubt about it, her mind and senses bright and taut. And the air tasted good. *First taste of freedom.*

Phoenix had said all along they had to be ready to move the moment the guard wasn't there. And he'd been right.

A face loomed out of the darkness. Phoenix, finger to lips. 'Don't move!' he whispered. 'Two on foot patrol.'

Phoebe held her breath. The crunch of boots on gravel rang crisp and crystal clear through the air. She touched her brother's arm. 'Relax,' she whispered. 'They're way off. Not going to hear us.'

Phoenix nodded, squeezed her hand then slithered away, silent as a shadow. At the roof's edge he slipped out of sight.

Phoebe followed, scuttling with the grace and supple speed of a gecko, down into the quadrangle. A cleaning

16

company truck stood in the corner by the gatehouse. Pressed flat against the walls, swiftly and without a sound, she crept her way closer in the shadows.

What was that? A door slammed. Voices. *The gatehouse?*

Dropping to the ground by the truck, Phoebe rolled between its wheels. Above her, jammed between two chassis struts, her brother grinned and winked. 'Just in time!'

Cleaning staff tramped past with their tools and other wheeled equipment in tow. Loading the gear into the back of the truck, they clambered on board. Weary, cheery voices, tired but glad to be going home at the end of a long shift.

Phoenix's eyes glinted in the confined gloom. 'Fasten your seat belts,' he hissed, 'for the ride of your life!'

Phoebe had been bracing herself for the engine, but when it started, the raw sound was like an explosion. It shook her violently, rattling her teeth and shivering the flesh on her bones. With a roar, the vehicle lurched. Beneath them the ground began to move. Her hands and feet, already numb from vibration, struggled to tighten their grip. Diesel exhaust swamped her lungs. Her stomach convulsed. The taste of vomit rose in her throat.

They were on their way. In a few minutes they would reach the tunnel entrance where guards checked the workers' papers. Then through and up the long driveway towards the massive outer fence and the main security gate.

It was late. Checks were slack. A torch beam sliced through the dark. A woman in uniform crouched and gave a cursory glance. There was yet another guard post to get through before they reached the main road. And beyond that, a drive to the border crossing for Portobello.

*

17

Something was wrong. In the time it had taken to drive to the border, had their escape been discovered? Guards were shouting at the driver. It was impossible to make out exactly what was being said, but their aggression carried clearly over the sound of the engine.

The single shot, into the ground behind the wheel, shook Phoebe to the core. The truck engine choked and died. She glanced at her brother. There was a new look in his eyes. Fear? He was listening intently.

'Out!' The sharp voice was edged with threat.

'Out? Why?'

'What have we done?'

'We've broken no laws.' From the truck the voices of frightened cleaners, men and women, pleading with the patrol.

'Why is this necessary? We've done nothing wrong.'

'Out! *Now!*' Another guard's voice. His anger reinforced by a second gunshot.

One by one, cleaners stepped from the truck.

Tucked away in the undercarriage, unable to see, Phoebe heard a dull thud and groan, followed immediately by the unmistakable crunch of body hitting ground. She coiled more tightly.

'Portobellan scum!' yelled a guard. 'Get up!'

A yelp of pain followed another sickening thud.

'Move it! Hurry!'

The remaining cleaners stumbled from the vehicle in panic.

'We could shoot you right here and now. Nobody would give a damn. Nobody would even know.'

'*Don't!*'

'Please – *no!*'

'We have families.'

'Please don't shoot!'

'Over there. With the others. Lie down. On the ground.'

There was a scurrying sound as cleaners obeyed orders. Then silence.

Phoebe glanced at her brother. He was frowning. She hoped he was thinking fast.

'Is that the last one?' barked a guard.

'Yes, sir.'

Phoebe held her breath.

'OK. Let them have it!'

Suddenly the truck began to shake, with a noise more deafening than the engine.

5

Mendel

The president was a manic depressive – his behaviour had always been unpredictable. Working at a high level within the Nebulese intelligence agencies, Mendel had spent enough time with him to know the signs well.

Over the last few weeks the president had undoubtedly entered a more volatile phase. Mendel sensed it was going to take all his manipulative skills, all his tact and diplomacy to steer the nation's supreme commander through the strategic minefield that now lay before them. Could he guide the president to a solution that might avoid international incident? More pressingly, could he hold the president's attention long enough for him to grasp even the rudiments of the problem?

Beneath his crisp, cool exterior, Mendel was sweating – he feared the answer to both these questions was a resounding No. 'Dr Kravitz and his team devote a great deal of time to monitoring the psychological development of their subjects. A while ago Kravitz expressed concern regarding "dysfunctional tendencies" exhibited by a couple of them.'

The president eyed the dossier in front of him. 'These twins?'

Mendel nodded.

'How was the guard killed?'

Mendel made a sharp twisting and snapping gesture with his hands. 'His neck, sir.'

'What? A highly trained ex-marine!' The president brought his fist down like a sledgehammer on the dossier. 'By one of these two . . . *children*!?'

'Yes, sir. We have to assume so. The body was dragged to a small storage room, here.' Mendel indicated the position on the floor plan. 'Unfortunately the camera in that corridor has been . . .'

'Let me guess,' grunted the president, wearily. 'Cleverly tampered with and rendered useless, like all the others?'

Mendel nodded. 'No footage.'

'Do we know how they got in the truck?'

'Yes, Mr President. Night-sight camera 129 remains intact. Its data block reveals the escapees concealing themselves beneath the vehicle.'

'Presumably they couldn't get at that camera because it was up some enormous pole?'

Mendel shrugged. 'More likely they just chose not to, sir. Perhaps they were short of time.'

The president gave a long sigh and sat back, arms folded. 'OK. What happened at the border crossing?'

'I'm not sure how to explain that, sir.'

'Try!' It was an order.

'They appear – somehow – to have taken control of the vehicle and driven it through the barrier.'

'In spite of small-arms fire from an *entire border patrol*?'

'Yes, sir. By all accounts the guard commander had been instructed to destroy the vehicle. The patrol had just finished disembarking the passengers when . . .'

'*Why?*' The president glared.

'I beg your pardon, sir?'

21

'Why didn't he just blow the damn thing up?'

'With all the cleaning staff still on board, Mr President?'

The president leant forwards. 'On a scale of one to ten, Mendel, how would you rate this incident in terms of threats to the future of our nation?'

Mendel nodded. 'Point taken, sir.'

'I would like words with the senior commander.'

'Yes, Mr President.'

'So where are they now, this boy and girl? Roaming free in Portobello?'

'The truck was peppered with hits before it even reached the barriers, sir. Apparently it ploughed on across no-man's-land, sideswiped a stationary vehicle, careened, struck a mine, flipped over four or five times and burst into flames.' Mendel cleared his throat. 'When our patrol arrived on the scene a few minutes later what was left of the truck was a raging inferno.'

The president frowned. 'Has the fire been extinguished?'

'Yes, sir. And so far no trace of the two escapees has been found.' Mendel bowed his head. 'We have to assume the worst.'

'What a cock-up!' The president rubbed his brow.

'We will find them, sir.'

'You're damn right we will, Mendel.' The president's face darkened. 'I'm ready to go in there right now with full military force. I will raze that whole Godforsaken city to the ground if that's what it takes!'

'Hopefully that won't be necessary, sir.'

'Necessary? I'm not interested in what's *necessary*!' The president shoved back his seat and got to his feet. 'That's the kind of thinking that got us into this mess.'

'Sir, with all due respect, an international incident at

this point in time would seriously hamper your negotiating position at the forthcoming World Trade Talks.'

'The forthcoming World Trade Talks?' The president's eyes bulged. His face darkened to the colour of overripe plums. 'Mendel, with all due respect, *I don't give a fig*! You are head of the national Security and Intelligence Agency, not Minister for Foreign Flipping Affairs. Kapeesh?'

Mendel bowed his head.

'I do *not* want to go down in history as the president who blew our nation's greatest opportunity to dominate the world!' With a sigh the president slumped back into his seat. 'I'm doubling naval and border patrols. All forces are on red alert. A week. I'll give you seven days, Mendel. Seven days for the SIA to clean up this mess or I'm going in. Is that understood?'

'Yes, sir.'

Tilting back his chair the president swung his legs up on to the desk. 'You must have given some thought to how you're going to tackle this.' He leant forward again. 'What do you have in mind? A Special Forces operation?' The eyes lit up. 'One of those surgical precision, lightning strikes?'

Mendel shook his head. 'That sort of operation is fine for eradicating terrorists, sir, but highly dependent on intelligence. And in this case, there's unlikely to be any.'

'What then?'

'I've been discussing our problem with Dr Kravitz.' Mendel took a dossier from his briefcase. Its cover bore two words: *Project Outcast*. He placed it on the desk. 'Mr President, I think I may have come up with a solution.'

6

Slubberdegullion

An hour after darkness, the freshly repaired barrier rose and a smart black government car sped through the checkpoint and across the stretch of no-man's-land. At the Portobellan border hut, an officer of the guard saluted and waved the sleek vehicle past the remains of a burnt-out truck.

By the time the car had crossed over into Portobello its number plates had altered to match the style of local issue. As had its headlights – one yellow now, one blue. And its rear lights – now both green. The vehicle was, to all intents and purposes, an official car of the Portobellan government. It purred on through empty streets and into the bustling heart of the city-state unimpeded.

Riding in air-conditioned comfort, cushioned by plush leather, Mendel gazed out through darkened glass. One after another, elegant office towers slid past, built on Portobellan soil but owned by Nebulese companies. The slim and gleaming NebEx building. Wider and taller, the NebBank. The shiny, soaring, silver NebTech. And so on. All of them, of course, were targets for terrorism, but strategically very important and extraordinarily well protected. Little by little Nebula was encroaching on Portobello. Appropriating it. One day, in the not too distant future, Portobellans would be left with just the rocky barren headland on which nothing grew or could be built.

But even that probably wouldn't defeat them.

A few blocks on, the squat inconsequential headquarters of the ramshackle Portobellan government drifted by. And further up the street, the missile- and bullet-scarred buildings that housed the so-called militia police and the various administrations.

The animosity between Nebula and Portobello had existed for so long no one could remember its origin. Two neighbouring tribes, two peoples, two nations locked together in bitter combat like savage dogs, relentlessly snarling and snapping at one another. Portobello – now nothing more than a small, mangy, mongrel. Nebula – a sleek, muscular mastiff. But exhausted and terribly wounded though Portobello was, with Nebula's jaws clamped to her bleeding throat and shaking her like a rag doll, she still showed no inclination to lie down and roll over.

Mendel scowled. To a problem solver like him, such an endlessly unresolved conflict was irksome. It pressed on a nerve. Reaching for his attaché case, he took out the Project Outcast dossier.

Kravitz had been a dark horse – deeply intelligent and, for a scientist, surprisingly easy to understand. But cagey as hell. Had he something to hide? Or was it just the nature of his work – dealing with such subterranean matters?

The project had received full clearance from the president and cooperation from Mendel's predecessor. Indeed the SIA had played an essential role in setting the whole thing up. Unfortunately, at an early stage the project had suffered a setback. Kravitz's colleague, who had been acting as the boy's mother in Portobello, had drowned in the storm wave that hit Downtown. Abandoned in that hostile world with no protection, the boy had been forced to fend for himself. He had gone feral.

Mendel peered at the grainy photograph of a man who had, more recently, taken the boy under his wing. Kravitz had described him as 'slippery and manipulative'. Cynically exploiting the city's internecine feuds for financial gain, this man had trained the boy to make the most of his unique talents, working for him. Delivering illicit packages across the city, breaking and entering, carrying out sabotage and surveillance, hunting down specified individuals. Some time ago the boy had graduated to assassinations. Intervention by Kravitz had been out of the question as any outside interference would have rendered the project meaningless.

Mendel was pinning his hopes on this boy and his misdirected talents giving them the edge on Kravitz's two escapees.

Despite state-of-the-art suspension, the car shook. Beyond the darkened windows labyrinthine Downtown, with its ramshackle buildings and narrow cobbled streets, shuddered past. The car cruised on towards the harbour with its acres of wharves and warehouses standing back to back in the gloom.

Here, down one of a hundred nameless and faceless streets, giant roller shutters lifted, the limousine drove through into darkness beyond, and the shutters clattered down again behind.

'My friend!'

Nodding for his bodyguards to wait by the car, Mendel made his way towards his beaming host. He returned the smile. It was important to show trust. The man appeared shorter and stouter than he'd imagined from the photograph. The thick head of hair had been slicked back and the face was now clean-shaven. But the aura of unctuousness remained.

'Good to meet you, my friend.' The man embraced him.

Mendel returned the gesture. 'Likewise.'

'Please –' The man indicated a table and two stools. 'Take a seat. Let us talk business. Tell me what you want. And I'll give you a price.'

'Refreshingly direct,' said Mendel. He seated himself. 'It makes these matters so much more straightforward.'

The man nodded, poured Mendel a glass of water, then sat back with his hands in his lap.

'I need someone finding,' said Mendel. 'Two people in fact.'

'I foresee no difficulty with that.'

Mendel studied the face in front of him. 'I might also need them to be killed . . .'

'That can be arranged too,' said the man. 'Unless, of course, they are the freedom fighters your people refer to as "terrorists".'

'No,' said Mendel. 'They are not.'

'Good. This city's too small.' The man shrugged apologetically. 'I am no supporter, but if I sent someone against the freedom fighters, they would know straight away. And I would be a dead man.'

'I understand.'

'Who is it you want to have killed?'

'That has to remain secret. I can, however, tell you they are Nebulese.'

Shock registered on the man's face. 'Here in Portobello?'

Mendel nodded. 'Illegally. This job will not be straight-forward but it will be well rewarded. I want the best you have.'

'Of course!' said the man. 'And I know just the right person. A boy, in fact.'

'A boy?' Mendel feigned surprise.

'Perhaps I should say – young man! A consummate professional. Sharp, resourceful and cunning.'

'This begins to sound promising.'

'But how will I instruct him, if you cannot instruct me?'

'I'll need to speak to your operative myself. Alone. I can explain directly to him what I need.'

'Then perhaps this particular boy is not right for the job. I have plenty of others, all very capable. Two or three spring immediately to mind.'

Mendel shook his head. 'This boy, you said, was the best.'

The man made an apologetic gesture with his hands. 'But I'm afraid he is fastidious about guarding his identity and he has always shunned contact with clients. He is also quite particular about which jobs he will and will not accept.'

Mendel considered for a moment. 'Perhaps you could send him on some small errand. I could meet him and speak to him. I'll explain what I need and he can decide for himself if he wants the job.'

The man's face twitched. 'I don't like this idea.'

'You will be well rewarded.'

'Rewarded! What use is money if I anger my best operative and lose his trust?'

Mendel shrugged away the objection. 'Perhaps we could put other work your way . . .' In spite of Kravitz's warnings, he had not expected this grasping slubberdegullion to be such hard work. 'The Nebulese government is always on the lookout for people they can work with.' He smiled rubbing his thumb against his fingertips. 'My bosses pay well for information . . . *very* well.'

The man's eyes twinkled. 'Now that starts to sound interesting! I suppose I could make out I'd sent the boy on some perfectly straightforward job . . .' He adopted an expression of surprise. 'I had no idea the client had been got at,' he said, practising the lie. 'I had no idea the SIA were lying in wait!' He leant forwards. 'You would make it clear to him, I didn't know you were going to do this?'

'Absolutely.'

'This I like!' He rubbed his hands greedily. 'OK. So before I give you a price, tell me . . . how do I get on this information payroll?'

7

Dolphins' Point

Crouching against a rock, Kai let his gaze drift across the bay. Silhouetted against the pure azure sky, an osprey glided, surveying its domain.

Its domain. But *his* whole universe. His prison. Everyone knew there was only one way out of Downtown: in a body bag.

From this furthermost tip of the headland, the metropolis appeared to be sliding into the sea. Buildings, and the spaces between them, grew smaller and more densely packed towards the lower slopes around the busy harbour. It gave the impression, and there was a good deal of truth in it, that the people down there near the water were being crushed by those who lived above.

Nebula on the higher ground, with its wide tree-lined boulevards, big comfortable houses and soaring towers. Crowded, crumbling Portobello below. Now Nebulese skyscrapers even stood on Portobellan land, over-shadowing the dark and narrow alleyways where he had grown up. The area known as Downtown. A busy harbour, surrounded by a chaotic mish-mash of densely packed tenements, cramped sweatshops and ugly factories that were, more often than not, foul-smelling. To say nothing of the people.

From the ground it was impossible to see where Portobello ended and Nebula began. The two cities merged into one. Shielding his eyes, Kai peered up into the sky. But from up there where the osprey was circling . . .

He rubbed scarred knuckles.

A concrete wall and high steel fencing, topped with electrified razor-wire, sliced between the two cities, from the precipitous rocky western shore to the beaches on the east. Fifty metres of open ground shadowed the entire length of the wall and fence on the Portobello side – a minefield, no-man's-land. Three roads leading to heavily fortified gates were the only routes through. All of that would be visible to a keen-eyed osprey.

But there were things that couldn't be seen, however high your vantage. Things it was hard to grasp even from the ground.

Like how, at this remarkable point, a city had stood in some shape or form for thousands of years. Before that, though, when the coastline had been differently shaped, there had been other ports, gateways to more ancient nations. These lay buried now under ever encroaching tides, lost to memory and history. But Kai knew. He had seen the evidence, deep beneath the waves.

And the way things were now, Portobello hemmed in and controlled by mighty Nebula, how had that come about? Having heard a thousand Portobellan versions of the story, Kai felt none the wiser. There was neither a sameness bonding each people, nor any real difference separating them that he could discern. And yet the Nebulese and Portobellans hated and mistrusted one another with a fierce intensity. Why was that? Historians could probably give an account of events that had led to this animosity, but could anybody honestly make sense of it? Or justify the consequences? He doubted it.

*

Kai's eyes narrowed as he returned his attention to the water. Searching, like the osprey, for telltale silhouettes. Already this morning he'd spotted several great whites. Where were the sharks now? Dogging the fishing fleet? Sniffing round the mouth of the harbour? Or down there, lurking beneath the reflected glare?

Bomm!

From across the water it had sounded like an explosion. He peered, waiting for smoke. But there was none. No more loud bangs either. Perhaps it had been the report of a gun. A single shot. Another death in Downtown.

A flash of white. The osprey was descending *fast*. Had it spotted something? Merciless and silent as a stone, it dropped from the sky, scarcely breaching the water. A flutter of wings and brief triumphant squawk, then it was rising again, prey flashing silver in its talons.

Kai watched the bird till it was a speck over the hills beyond the city. Only when it had completely vanished from sight did he return his attention to the sea. Now it was time to decide. Dive from this side and take his chance with the sharks? Or climb the short path to the top of the ridge and risk a swim with *the beast*?

Without checking the position of the sun or calculating, Kai knew instinctively it was too late. While he'd been letting his mind wander, time had unravelled. On the far side of the promontory, the she-monster would already be growling with hunger. Pulling off his boots, he stripped to his trunks, belt and holster. Medusa would have to wait. It'd be throwing away life to risk those waters now the tide had turned.

Undoing the catch on the holster, he took out his new gun. New to him, but old, worn and clunky. The furtive, black-market dealer, a woman who knew all about weapons, had assured him it was designed to fire under water and could easily hit a target with deadly force. And at more than fifty metres. There was a catch, however. The ammunition it required was not only special and very expensive, but the gun was a breech loader and could only fire one shot at a time.

Hardly satisfactory but better than nothing. It was a start. Taking one of the large cartridges from his pouch, he opened the breech and slotted it home. With the gun back in the holster, he was ready.

Making his way down to the ledge, he located the small flat area of rock he had selected as a diving platform. Its angular edge was well defined. Shaking himself, he loosened every joint and sinew before standing square, feet together and flat on the rock. He centred himself, gripped the edge with his toes and retightened, muscle by muscle. A quick glance at the ocean, forty metres below, and a final, clear visualization of what he was about to attempt. Then a long, slow, deep intake of breath . . . last one for a while.

Up on toes, holding the balance, he waited. He liked to stretch this moment. But it made him uneasy being in full, if distant, view of the harbour and passing ships. With the merest tilt of his head he started the chain reaction. Gravity, ever so lightly, pulling him forwards. As he keeled, he gave at the knees, arms moving back in counter-balance. Then, at the right moment, an explosive spring from the toes and . . . *away*! Head raised. Arms outstretched. Flying. Out across a mosaic of glistening turquoise and gold. Down towards the rising waves . . .

Lower head.

Snap arms together. Straight as an arrow.

The sea hurtling up to meet . . .

33

Splooosh!

The shock of the cold was intense. But by the time he had slowed to a halt, held weightless by water several metres down, his body had adjusted. He peered up at the shimmering surface and his fast vanishing trail of bubbles. The velocity of all that falling, absorbed by so little water – it amazed him every time.

There was plenty of light at this depth and Kai's eyes were already adjusting to the changed element. Because the sea bed was largely rock, the water here would always remain clear except in the most extreme conditions. Reorienting himself, he made a quick swivel to get his bearings then set off with a strong kick and wide slow strokes.

He knew the route by heart. Across to the pinnacle. Down to the shelf. Then follow the crack to the small cluster of coral. The crack was long; he counted the strokes, twenty-six, twenty-seven, twenty-eight! He was pulling well. Two fewer than last time.

Could he really do it all on one lungful? All that practising. All that training. All that working on technique. Stretching himself, little by little. Pushing his limits.

Keep relaxed. Keep the mind focused, that was the thing. Banish doubt.

Passing the coral, he swung a sharp left. The shelf dropped steeply here. Now he could see his target – the enormous, shellfish-encrusted, bronze head, half buried in sand. A relic of some earlier civilization, its one eye, just visible, watched his approach.

The sea bed was littered with ruins, wrecks and boulders. Sponges, crustaceans and all manner of underwater life had gathered. Shoals of anchovies and sardines shimmered like one giant organism as they tacked first one way then the other. Larger, more colourful fish he recognized but couldn't name, nosed amongst the broken stone columns of some ancient building. But not a barracuda or shark in sight. Too early yet to be grateful.

Water pressure was ringing in his ears. It hurt. The bones of his skull creaked and shifted, adjusting. Reassuringly, they always did at this point. Pulling himself still lower, maintaining the rhythm of his strokes, he glided in towards the sunken head, patted it one, two, three times, then, at the same steady pace, set off back.

Half-way.

Rhythm was important for holding breath underwater. Rhythm lulled the brain. Quelled panic. It was important now not to squander what little air remained. A desperate attempt to sprint for the finishing line could blow everything. Time to focus . . .

One, two, three . . .

Count and maintain a steady rhythm . . .

nine, ten, eleven . . .

Swing past the coral clusters. Pull and kick, pull and kick . . .

twenty-five, twenty-six, twenty-seven . . .

The long stretch. Don't be tempted to rise. Just keep going . . .

forty-eight, forty-nine, fifty!

Kai exhaled the last portion of stale air from his lungs. The bubbles shimmered and wobbled, up and away. Now he was on absolute empty, but he was rising too, his skull creaking, his lungs burning and muscles leaden. Beyond caring about counting, or numbers.

An enormous shoal of mackerel engulfed him, silver wisps and flashes streaming past with scarcely a touch as he pushed on, up over the shelf, kicking and pulling with all his might towards the pinnacle. Now there was real urgency about his movements. Above, the refracted sun, a big splash of light, jiggled and stretched as he soared towards it. Up, up, up like a rocket.

'Heeaaaaaaaaargh!'

Yes! Sunlight burned his eyes as he breached the surface. About twenty metres from the cliff. Near enough the spot where he'd entered the sea. *Perfect.* Treading water, he sucked in lungfuls of sweet-tasting air. Relief. Pride. Euphoria.

Muscles began to tingle and glow. He had done it! Swum the distance. Of course, it would be a hundred times more difficult when he did it for real. Over on the other side. There would be impossible currents, murky darkness, heaven only knew what else . . .

Lying back, he allowed the water to take the weight of his head. Then torso and legs too. Waves rolled under him to crash, moments later, against the rocks beyond. A sense of deep relaxation washed over him. Hard to resist. But he knew he had to fight it. This was the most dangerous time. This was when he was most vulnerable. There could be no relaxing till . . .

Suddenly, he was alert and rigid. Through his toes, not a hundred metres off, a dark shape was rising beneath the waves at astonishing speed. *A great white.* Unmistakable. And cutting a line straight towards him.

In one movement, he reached for the holster, undid the catch and wrenched out the gun. Raising it above his head, he submerged himself in a clumsy feet-first dive.

The shark was closing. Gripping the gun with two hands, he extended his arms ready to aim.

Booom.

There was a flash. A tearing pain in his shoulder. Stinging saltwater ripped up through his sinuses. The underwater world spun. Something hard crashed against his knee. A tail shape sliced across his vision. And then he was groping for the surface, gasping for air.

Instinct cut in. With three explosive porpoise kicks, Kai launched himself towards the cliffs. Flinging arms forwards in a deep butterfly stroke, he pulled and kicked with all his might. The shore was close and a wave was rising. In a desperate burst of strength he pushed his speed to match the wave's. With a surge, its momentum picked him up, held him and carried him forwards. He was rising too, no longer even kicking. His taut horizontal body hurtling forwards in a sheer wall of water . . . towards the rocks.

8

Reunion

Panting as he neared the top, Kai glanced down at the cove below. The unmistakable silhouettes were still there, five of them circling just a small distance from the breakers. Could they still smell fear though he was this far above them?

So much for the gun.

The water had dried on his body as he climbed. The torn muscle in his left shoulder throbbed. The gashes on his chest from the rocks had already started to crust. Brushing salt from his abdomen, he turned to the rock face, gripped the granite hard and hauled himself scrabbling up the final stretch.

'Incr-cr-credible!'

Looking up with a start, Kai scowled at the plump, straight-haired boy propped against a rock. Clod. 'What are you doing here?' He was holding a bundle. Kai recognized the items. 'With *my* clothes?'

Clod blushed. 'Sorry,' he blurted, shuffling awkwardly. 'I f-f-folded them for you.' He nodded towards the water. 'That was impressive.' With his familiar twisted gait, he stepped forwards, lurching from side to side, swivelling his pelvis to drag his lame foot. 'You were underwater an unb-b-believable length of time. How did you do that?'

'Held my breath.'

'But it was easily f-f-five minutes! More, I'm s-s-sure.'

Kai shrugged. 'I'm a natural. And I practise.' Swimming anywhere other than Portobello beach was illegal. Anywhere else the waters were so dangerous people seldom tried unless they were suicidal or attempting escape, which amounted to the same thing. So it was best no one knew what he was up to. He glared at Clod. 'Keep quiet about this, understood?'

Clod gave a nervous, bird-like nod.

Snatching the neat pile of clothes, Kai let them drop to the ground in a heap. He began dressing. 'How on earth did you get up here, anyway?'

'Very, very s-s-slowly!' Clod was trying to lighten the mood. 'It took me the b-b-best part of half a day!' He looked away. 'After you just v-v-vanished, we started to worry something b-b-bad had happened.'

In a flash Kai had Clod by the throat. 'Did you tell anyone?'

'No!' Clod trembled. 'Not a s-s-soul.'

Kai searched Clod's eyes for signs of deception.

'Not even my f-f-father,' squealed Clod. 'I swear! I said "w-w-we" but I meant "I". I was the one who was w-w-worried.'

Kai let go. 'Sorry . . .' He shook his head, grabbed his boots off Clod and handed him his wet trunks.

Clod massaged his neck. 'I thought maybe you'd l-l-lost your nerve.'

Shoving his feet down hard inside the leather, Kai threw Clod a scowl.

'But from wh-what I've just witnessed d-d-down there,' Clod added hastily, 'it's obvious you've n-n-not!'

Kai's scowl faded. 'I feel strong. Better than I can remember.'

Clod looked sceptical. 'Have you been l-l-living out here?'

Nodding, Kai inhaled deeply and noisily through his nostrils. 'Fresh sea air! Good for body and soul.' Taking back his trunks, he wrung them out and looped them through his belt. 'I know why you've come, Clod.'

'I w-wanted to m-make sure you were OK.'

'Perhaps . . .' Kai smiled. He could read Clod like a book. 'But Paps has sent you to find me, hasn't he? There's another job.'

Clod squirmed.

'Well, the answer is no.' Kai could see in Clod's face he suspected this was loss of nerve. 'Clod, have you ever seen me terrified?'

Clod's face twitched. He stared at the ground.

'It's OK. You can answer truthfully.'

'In that derelict ap-p-partment,' Clod struggled with his own nerves, 'after the ass-ass-ass . . .'

'Assassination?'

'Thank you. You s-s-seemed pretty sc-sc-scared of something.'

Kai looked into Clod's eyes. *Tell him?* 'I heard a sound. The same sound I heard as a small child. No one else could hear it when I was young. I remember being patted on the head, and grown-ups telling me I was imagining things. Ma even worried I had an ear infection.' He chuckled but shook his head gravely. 'No one, it seems, can hear it this time round either. Perhaps I'm imagining it again.'

'What kind of s-s-sound? You said before it was the s-s-sound of Death?'

Kai nodded. 'Short bursts of a deep, strangled, groaning sound, coming from below the ocean, out there.' He pointed towards the horizon. 'Remember the killer wave that hit Downtown when we were small?'

'The st-st-storm wave!' Clod nodded, wide-eyed. 'Oh G-G-God, I'm sorry.' He tutted and dug his knuckles into his thighs. 'Your m-m-mother . . .'

Staring out to sea, Kai nodded. His mother had been one of the many who had drowned that day. Having taken him to safety on a roof, she had dashed back down to the street to grab a child she had spotted standing there, staring in terror at the approaching wave. Kai had watched the wave crash down on them. That was the last he'd ever seen of her.

With a deep shuddering breath, he pushed the memory away. 'I think the strange groaning sounds I heard back at that time were a forewarning of the wave. I was the only one who heard them. They came before it and, in the weeks leading up to it, grew more and more frequent. After the wave struck, I never heard them again.' He looked at Clod. 'Until now. Until that time a few weeks ago.'

'When I th-th-thought you were going crazy?' said Clod. 'Or had been hit by a b-b-bullet?'

Kai nodded.

'This is incr-cr-credible!'

'It's exactly the same sound.'

'No wonder you were so sh-sh-shaken.' Clod looked at him curiously. 'Perhaps it's the s-s-sea's anger! What if you're r-r-right?'

Picking up a small stone, Kai hurled it out over the ocean. He watched it arc, fall and disappear into the water. 'Another storm wave is on its way.'

9

Petrified

Negotiating the steep descent from Dolphins' Point had been no simple matter. In spite of his strength and fitness, Kai was feeling drained. The exhilaration of the dive and swim had worn off and his shoulder was aching. Clod was ungainly more than heavy, his lame leg had made it hard work negotiating the twists and turns. Several times they had nearly fallen. Having finally reached the flatter section, where the path meandered across the ridge, Kai paused to rest.

'Let me g-g-get this right,' Clod made himself comfortable on a boulder. 'You plan to *leave*?'

Kai nodded. 'Bodysurfing the rebound from the storm-wave.'

Clod laughed and tapped his skull. 'First you're hearing the ocean's growls. Now you're t-t-telling me you think you can *escape*. And by riding a giant w-w-wave?'

'My mind is crystal clear. Never been clearer.'

Clod shook his head. 'Bodysurfing a rebound wave is the cr-craziest idea I ever h-h-heard!'

Kai shrugged. 'You'd better get used to it. It's what I'm going to do.'

'You plan to just st-st-stay out here,' said Clod, 'w-w-waiting for your wave?'

'Believe me,' said Kai, 'it won't be long.'

'But how will you l-l-live? You look th-th-thinner already. Do you eat?'

'I've made the odd trip into Downtown,' said Kai. 'And I'll make another yet before I leave. There's a certain gun dealer I need to talk to.' His hand moved, quick as a flash, snatching at something that scuttled by his feet.

Clod flinched, startled. 'What's th-th-that?'

Kai held out his catch for inspection. 'Head . . . thorax . . . abdomen . . . and six wriggling legs. *Periplaneta orientalis.*' He chuckled. 'Tasty cockroach!'

Clod looked horrified. 'You eat *those*?'

'Hmmm!' Kai licked his lips. 'Very nutritious.' As he popped it in his mouth, Clod blanched and turned away. 'Delicious too!'

Clod squirmed at the crunching sound and covered his ears. After a few moments the crunching was replaced by laughter; curiosity got the better of him and he turned back to peek.

'Too, too easy!' Kai opened his mouth wide to show it was empty. Making the chewing sounds again, he thrust his fist towards Clod and opened it.

'The c-c-cockroach!'

'Still whole,' said Kai, 'and wriggling with vitality! What do you take me for, Clod? You think I'd eat one of these?' He chuckled. '*Raw?*' Tossing the creature aside, he nodded towards the sea. 'That's my larder.'

Still scowling and pouting at being tricked, Clod looked out across the bay. 'Is Portobello really so b-bad that you have to l-l-leave?'

'Looks pretty from a distance,' said Kai, 'but it's no place to live. I've never felt at home there. Fenced in and kept at a distance from the land of milk and honey. Surrounded on all other sides by lethal waters.'

He spat at the ground. 'Portobello is worse than a prison.'

'Don't you th-th-think that's a little harsh?'

Kai shook his head. 'There's nowhere to go. No money or work. People fight amongst themselves, robbing and killing each other over nothing.' He snorted. 'Harsh? I don't think so.'

Clod shrugged.

'The freedom fighters,' said Kai, 'strike some pathetic blow against the Neb oppressor, and our whole city's medical supplies are cut off in retaliation. Small children, the sick and infirm die. Another futile attack, and Downtown suffers a more violent retribution. Old people, women and children are *collateral*, maimed and killed in bloody reprisals.'

Clod glanced self-consciously at his leg. 'I heard an explosion earlier.'

Kai shrugged. 'Just another day in Downtown.'

'That stretch of water,' said Clod, pointing towards the sea, 'is probably the most sh-sh-shark-infested in the world.'

'I know.' Kai nodded. In the open sea beyond Dolphins' Point, one of the swift Nebulese navy ships that patrolled the waters day and night was cruising. 'They keep it that way. It serves their purpose.'

'But even if your st-st-storm wave were to happen,' said Clod, 'do you really th-th-think you stand a chance?'

'I'm leaving,' said Kai. 'My mind's made up.'

Prevailing winds were off the ocean to the west. But centuries of visitors to Dolphins' Point had favoured comfort over spectacle and so the path worn by their feet made its way, not across the ridge top, but in the shelter of the eastern slope. It was only where the ridge came to an end that the headland began to make its final descent into Downtown. Here, beyond the ridge's final pinnacle, the path emerged once more into the prevailing winds on the low rounded summit of Gorgon's Rest.

Here there was no protection from the wind sweeping in off the ocean. Bracing himself against its force Kai paused to allow Clod to catch up. Always, he felt exhilarated in this wild place. The tang of ozone, the buffeting wind, Medusa's roar ... Who could reach here and not feel drawn to the west side, the headland's other face?

'Sc-sc-scares me to death!' Clod had to yell to make himself heard over the sound.

Kai nodded. 'Me too!' With every step the roar grew louder. His gut was clenched now. A mixture of terror and exhilaration. 'Come on!' He paused to take Clod's arm once more. 'Lean into it!' There was no shelter here. Just an old stone plinth, waist high and battered by the elements. The gale was spitting seaspray and gusting strongly enough to blow a fully grown man to the ground.

Ocean. Vast, cobalt blue, open. Though Kai had come to this place countless times before, his heart galloped in excited anticipation of what lay beyond the edge. The roar was deafening. He felt Clod's grip tighten as the first white wraiths became visible.

With a fine seaspray drenching their faces, Kai narrowed his eyes and dragged Clod stumbling forwards, battling against the squally onslaught. Ahead of them spume leapt high into the racing wind.

Clod's resistance grew heavier; he was trembling. His mouth moved. But any sound he may have uttered was snatched away by the wind or drowned by roar. Kai coaxed him forwards gently, step by step towards the edge, towards the she-monster in all her terrifying beauty. 'Come *on*!' he urged. 'Just a couple more steps!'

Clod, like most Portobellans, clearly did not share Kai's enthusiasm for the spectacle.

'Have courage!'

'I can't!' Clod had stopped dead. He shook his head. 'I ought to be g-g-getting back . . .'

'Just a few more moments.' Kai put an arm around him. 'Nearly there!' As he eased him forwards, the whole ocean seemed suddenly to churn and surge below them. Clod's hands clutched him tight. '*Behold!*' yelled Kai.

Clod gawped at the writhing sea serpents, vicious and venomous, spitting and snapping. Wide-eyed and slack-jawed with horror, he took in the terrible vision: the enormous, omnipotent ocean being sucked into a furious, spiralling frenzy.

'Magnificent!' yelled Kai.

Truly awesome. *Medusa*. Portobello's seething, dark and deadly monster. The largest, most powerful and most destructive whirlpool on the planet. Rolling, cavernous and immense, she gaped and roared with a dizzying sound like the crushing of mountains. And all around her, the agitated ocean swirled, boiled, churned.

Clod still gaped. He had turned to stone.

Nudging him, Kai nodded towards the ocean. 'This is the side I'm leaving from.'

'What?' Clod shook himself from his trance. 'What are you s-s-saying? You're going off h-h-here!?' He took a step back from the precipice. 'Into th-th-there? Into . . .' He pointed, his hand shaking. 'Into . . . into *that*?' His face had drained of colour. 'Are you m-m-mad? N-no one could survive!'

Kai nodded. 'You're right, I think, without the storm wave.' He grinned. 'Though better to die here in the maw of Medusa than on the other side, torn apart by great whites!'

Clod narrowed his eyes against the awful vision. 'Talk to Paps,' he yelled. 'P-p-please?'

Kai shook his head. 'I'm done with all that. I've finally found a way out.'

'I h-h-have to get back,' said Clod. 'But please c-consider it. One last j-j-job?' Stumbling as he turned, he clutched Kai's sleeve for support. 'He really needs you!'

Kai chuckled. 'I doubt it. There are plenty of others keen for the work.'

'But you're the b-b-best!'

'Maybe,' said Kai. 'But poor Paps'll just have to make do. That part of my life is over. I'm no longer for hire.'

10

Dead People Talk

Portobello's daily market was to be found in the main piazza, Downtown, just a short walk from the harbour. From soon after dawn every morning except holy days and holidays, market traders cried their wares in full voice, competing with one another, counterpointing one another.

'Rat-traps!'

'Lovely bags! Bags with loads of room in!'

'Capsicums!'

'Hats and caps!'

'Camomile and cumin!'

Parallel rows of stalls ran the entire length of the square. There were hundreds, selling everything from fresh herbs to smelling salts, from cured fish to pickled thrush, from cooking pots to bolts of brightly coloured cloth. The whole of Portobello came here to shop.

On the periphery, beggars hovered. The young, scavenging in packs. The old, crippled and sick, propped against walls, arms outstretched, their lined and crumpled faces maps of suffering and dejection.

Pushing his way through the crowds Kai strode purposefully across the piazza. The particular dealers he was looking for kept their goods hidden. There were always lookouts posted at either end of the street. These stalls were all discreetly guarded.

'Well, well, well! If it isn't the reprobate of all Downtown!' Tight brown ponytail and watchful chestnut eyes. Combat fatigues and freedom fighter headband. Clutching an armful of pamphlets, Topaz looked formidable. She smiled. 'Haven't seen you around for a while.'

Kai halted. 'Hey! My favourite girl soldier.'

'Shopping?'

'Killed anyone today?'

The smile became a scowl. 'Forever trying to provoke me!'

'What?' protested Kai. 'Me!? Never! On my honour!'

'You have no honour.'

'Ooh!' Kai clutched his heart. 'So harsh!'

'Sarcasm and cynicism do nothing for you.'

'How you misjudge me,' said Kai. 'It was meant sincerely.'

'Really.' Topaz looked around, as if taking in for the first time where she was and the kind of items traded. 'And what would a young boy like you be trying to buy in Firearms Alley?'

'Would you believe – an umbrella?'

Topaz shook her head.

'OK . . .' Kai leant close, conspiratorial, his voice a whisper. 'As you can see, I'm empty handed. But I was actually trying to buy . . .' he glanced around, mock-surreptitiously, 'a *gun*.'

'You don't say.'

'I'm after a particular sort. A few days ago there were several for sale but, strangely, today nobody has what I need.'

'Who're you going to shoot?'

'Sshh!' Kai put a finger to his lips. 'I don't shoot people. This was for a shark.'

'They're all sharks of one kind or another, aren't they, the people you associate with?'

'Shark as in fish.'

'Oh, really?' Topaz laughed. 'Next you'll be trying to persuade me you want to join the PFF.'

'Me? A Portobellan Freedom Fighter? I don't think so.'

'Your skills are wasted.' Topaz waved a pamphlet under Kai's nose. 'We could put them to good use. There's a war going on.'

Kai looked around. 'Where?'

'Our people are being killed every day.'

'*Our* people?' Kai shook his head. 'Would that include the "sharks" you just mentioned?' He gestured at the people milling around them. 'All I see is a city full of stupid, greedy animals fighting amongst themselves for worthless scraps.'

'You don't see oppression?'

'Of course I do. I'm not blind. But I also see a headstrong, thinks-she's-tough girl, full of rage, throwing in her lot with a bunch of would-be revolutionaries, desperate to sacrifice themselves as quick as they can for pie in the sky ideals and glory.'

'*Thinks*-she's-tough!?' Topaz took a step forwards. 'That's a joke, coming from you.' She leant closer, attempting to intimidate. 'Let me tell you something, Mr I'm-such-a-bigshot-I-hang-around-with-crooks-and-gangsters . . .'

Kai laughed out loud. 'What am I supposed to do? Who in this city is neither crook nor gangster?'

Topaz ignored him. 'Ideals are *by definition* pie in the sky.' She jabbed him with her finger. 'They're *ideal*, stupid.

They're something to aim for and strive towards. You don't get more liberty truffling in the dirt, feathering your own nest, sitting around on your butt watching the world go by. Or whatever else it is you do. It's all about *struggle*.'

'In this city, you don't get more liberty *full stop*.'

'By banding together to fight the Neb oppressor, the people of Portobello will.'

'Will? Will when? You're spouting! Your group and others like you have been struggling for as long as anyone can remember. And spouting even longer. And are the people of Portobello one tiny bit more free? I don't think so.'

'If people hadn't fought and made sacrifices on our behalf,' said Topaz, 'who knows how much worse things might be?'

'So things being this good is down to you lot.'

Topaz shot him a thunderous look. 'You're arrogant, pig-headed, selfish . . .'

Kai winked, '. . . but you love me!'

Her arm swung but he caught the hand before it struck.

'Let *go*!' Topaz tugged hard. Pamphlets went whirling into the air as she whacked him with her other hand. 'You deluded ape!'

Though she struggled Kai held firm. A few faces turned.

Topaz's eyes flashed fury. 'You think you know everything!'

'I know you.'

'Huh! You do not!' Topaz clawed at his fingers. 'Leave go, or I'll make a scene.'

'I thought you already were doing.' Kai smiled. 'I meant love as in *brotherly* love. You know, like growing up playing in the same streets together?'

Topaz scowled, but the fight was already leaching out of her.

Kai relaxed his grip.

Topaz rubbed her wrist. 'How differently we turned out.'

'Yeah.'

'Don't you ever stop to think about what you do? Doesn't it bother you?'

Kai shrugged. 'What I do is *my* business.'

'I know what you do, Kai. People talk. I know what you get up to.'

'You should take what people say with a big pinch of salt. Most of it's poisonous swill.'

'What d'you think your mother would say?'

'The same as every other dead mother – nothing.'

'Don't you have a conscience?'

'No!' Kai's eyes were like green lasers. 'I don't believe in conscience. I don't believe in God. And I certainly don't believe in politics – your stupid variety or anybody else's.' People were staring. His voice grew louder as he vented anger. 'Family? Hah! What's family? And as for love – love is the biggest lie of all!' Sidestepping Topaz, he strode off, barging his way angrily through the crowded market.

'You're just a boy,' yelled Topaz. 'Just a boy, and already you believe in *nothing*?'

'I believe in one thing.'

'What's that?'

'*Me!*'

11

Unnatural

A mist had descended. A fog of fury. He had stormed through the crowds, blind to where he was going. Ranting inside his head. Replaying the things Topaz had said that so incensed him. Opening the wound again and again. Stoking the rage.

He knew he was right. He was what he was. Had never been anything else. And why should he want to be? He was him. An outsider. He had grown up alone. Alone was what he did. And what he did best. Why did she question that? Why did she try to change him? Why did she make him so angry? How *dare* she?

There was a bottleneck in the crowd. People were so densely packed, Kai was forced to abandon his thoughts to probe for a way through.

'It is coming!' A familiar screechy voice carried over the hubbub of the people. 'The wave is coming! Hark! Do you not hear?'

The wave? Kai's interest was pricked. It was the voice of Mushirah, a wandering blind woman, as much a feature of Downtown as the narrow cobbled streets, the market and the harbour. He had seen her sometimes, on the beach, on the harbour wall, on the headland coves, standing for hours facing out towards the ocean. What was she doing then? Listening to the waves? Smelling the brine? Thinking?

Some days, Mushirah was full of dark, doomladen prophecy. Others, she brimmed with bright, babbling nonsense. In between she watched the world through eyeless sockets. Many locals spoke of her with reverence as a prophet and seer. Many more mocked her as mad. Sceptical to the core, Kai had always given her the widest berth possible.

As he pushed and ducked his way through, it became apparent that Mushirah was the cause of the bottleneck. Standing still as a statue against the street corner, with a small space around her, she cupped her ear and craned her neck. 'O busy, bustling, denizens of Downtown, rest one moment and listen.'

A squint-eyed youth, taller and older than Kai, stepped out of the crowd and took Mushirah's hand. 'I hear it, Grandmother! I hear it!' With a big idiot grin for his captive audience, the youth turned, stuck out his arse and let rip. The crowd rewarded his impressive flatulence with loud laughter and cheers. But Mushirah shook her head disparagingly. 'The terrible time is almost upon us. Waste not your days in idle mockery, trivial toil or slumber. But put yourselves to the purpose. Prepare! Prepare!'

Shaking their heads, the main part of the gathered crowd began to disperse. They had more important things to attend to. There was bartering and haggling to be done.

Kai remembered Mushirah from his youngest days. Those eyeless sockets that seemed to see everything had always held a fear and fascination for him. Even now, though Mushirah had turned to speak to a young woman who had approached her for a consultation, Kai felt as though her attention was somehow on him. The old fear was stirring, tinged with a reluctant curiosity.

From the other side of the street, Kai watched Mushirah

place a hand on the woman's face. He had seen this done before, by her and others who, like her, claimed to have mystical powers. They gave readings – analysed an individual's character and prospects, made predictions, offered advice.

Kai felt a shiver travel down his spine. Though Mushirah's face was turned away and she had bent to mutter to the woman, her arm slowly extended, unravelling like a snake towards him. A finger beckoned. Kai glanced around. People were chattering indifferently amongst themselves or gazing at market stalls. Mushirah was summoning him.

'Thank you, Grandmother.' Placing a small coin in Mushirah's hand, the young woman picked up her shopping and scurried off.

Mushirah turned and gave Kai a crooked smile. 'You're wondering if I have eyes hidden behind these empty sockets.' Her laugh was part cackle, part babbling brook. She shook her head. 'Eyes are not the only organ of sight.' Again the finger beckoned. 'Come closer.' She opened her mouth wide. 'Look – no teeth! I'm a frail old woman. I will not bite!'

Kai approached, glad nobody seemed to be paying either of them any attention. It felt as if invisible fingers had stretched out from Mushirah's mind and were somehow probing his. She sensed what he was thinking. She knew what he was feeling. He didn't like it.

'Let me touch your face, child.' Mushirah placed her hand on his brow. 'I knew your mother.'

Kai felt the hairs stand up on the back of his neck. He still hadn't spoken a word. Did she somehow recognize him?

'She used to bring me food,' said Mushirah. 'It saddened

me deeply when she was taken from us.' She waited, head cocked as though expecting a reply. When Kai said nothing, she leant close and sniffed at his skull. 'Hmmm. Taciturn!' She smiled to herself and nodded. 'Testing me . . .'

The fingers followed the contours of his face, gently but firmly probing into every space – the corners of his eyes, the bottom of his nostrils, between his lips, intruding even inside his ears. It was hard not to squirm.

'The wave that took her is returning. You know this to be true.'

How could Mushirah know? Had she heard the sounds too?

'The time is close. You dream of escape. But you are not ready. There is something that you need. And there are things you must do before leaving.'

What something? A gun? . . . *And what things?* Loose ends to tie up? Preparations to make? Unforeseen things?

The urge to question was as strong as the urge to recoil. Kai stood clenched and silent. He was his own master. A free agent. He thought for himself and took advice from no one. Mushirah's words might seem to hold truth, but how could she know this? Clever intuition? Invention? A trick to dupe him? The doubting part of his mind coiled, ready to spring.

'Your mother's name was Ana.'

'No!' Instinctively Kai pulled away. Lies!

Mushirah's other hand pressed against his back. 'Oh, but it was! You couldn't have known. Rüya never told a soul.'

Rüya! Kai gave an involuntary gasp. Mushirah knew his mother's name! She knew his mother. And therefore knew who he was. His mind reeled. 'I don't understand. My mother had a second name? A secret name?'

56

Mushirah shrugged. 'I can tell you no more than that. A fine woman. A sanguine woman. There is much of her in you.' The fingers continued their probing. More slowly now, as if creeping over every pore, stroking every hair for clues. 'I met you when you were only small. A baby.'

'I don't remember.'

'I never forget. I felt it then but . . .' Her voice trailed away.

'Felt what?'

Mushirah frowned. 'You are unlike any I have met.'

'Isn't everybody different?'

'Of course.'

'Then I don't understand.'

'The world and everything it contains is made up of four elements – earth, water, air and fire, each expressed in humours – blood, choler, phlegm and melancholy. In each of us, one is dominant. But in you I sense all four quite clearly and distinctly. In exactly equal parts. A complete balance. And there is something else I cannot fathom . . .'

'And is all this good? Or bad?'

'Unnatural.'

12

Green Star Noodle Bar

Paps wiped his mouth, slapped his paunch and belched.

Leaning past the fat belly, Clod gingerly reached for the platter his father had just shoved away. It was the third he had consumed in this one sitting. Paps always ate when he was agitated or angry. Had his rage finally been soaked up by the food?

Fat chance.

Big hand grabbed smaller wrist. 'Where is he, then? Where is the boy?' Paps jerked Clod round to face him. 'You had better not disappoint me.'

Clod shrank back but no blow came. 'I've t-t-tried my best. It took a long t-t-time even to track him down.'

Paps slapped the table. 'And then the ingrate said no! After all the work I've put his way!'

'I'm sure he didn't m-mean to snub you, Pa-pa-pa-pa.'

'Huh.' Paps pulled the boy close. 'That's the way I'll take it, if he lets me down. I've made a commitment to a *very special client*.'

Whispered on foul breath, the significance of these last words was not lost on Clod. His father had returned from that secret meeting in a state of considerable agitation, ranting about Kai. Now Clod had an inkling of why. 'H-h-hopefully,' he said, 'my plan will w-w-work.'

'Hopefully? It had better!'

'You need to be p-p-patient,' Clod trembled. 'Give it t-t-time.'

Tightening his grip, Paps pressed a hamlike fist against his son's cheek. 'If I bought those useless old guns off those thieving market traders for no reason . . .'

'Ow!' There were tears in Clod's eyes. 'Kai will c-c-come to you. He has to.'

'That's right!' Paps squeezed the wrist. 'You useless, stuttering *cripple*!'

Clod squealed.

Customers glanced up from their food but carried on eating. Paps raising hand or voice to his hapless son was an unremarkable event.

But Clod was hopping up and down, jabbering and pointing with his free hand. 'K-K-K . . .' On the piazza in front of the restaurant, he had spotted a familiar shape emerging from the crowds. 'K-K-K . . . !'

Before Paps could swivel his bulk, Kai had loped inside and bounced up the short flight of steps. He strolled to where they were seated. 'Paps!'

'Kai?' Paps rose. 'Kai, my boy!'

Slim boy and portly man embraced one another like long-lost friends.

Clod breathed a sigh of relief.

'This warms my heart!' Paps beamed magnanimously at Kai. 'You know you're like a son to me!'

There was cynicism in Kai's chuckle. 'And you, Paps, are the father I never had.'

'Are you hungry?' asked Paps. 'You look hungry.'

'Always does,' chimed Clod.

'Don't you eat?' Paps squeezed Kai's upper arm. The biceps was slim but solid. 'Are your visits here the only time you get food?' He snapped his fingers at his son. 'Fetch the house special.'

Clod's eyes met Kai's. 'Would sir like a d-d-drink with that?'

Kai had a smile for Clod. He nodded. 'The usual.'

'C-c-coming right up.'

As Clod lurched his way towards the kitchens, Paps snapped his fingers again. 'Hey! Make sure you bring extra firebeans.'

Clod ducked his head and vanished through the bead curtain.

'Come.' Paps put his hand on Kai's shoulder. 'Sit with me. Let's talk.'

The Green Star Noodle Bar was always crowded. Kai followed Paps as he threaded his way through the busy restaurant, greeting his customers with a nod, a laugh, a smile of crooked yellow teeth, a joke. On the veranda overlooking the bustling market place, they sat at the table Paps reserved for special guests and private business meetings.

'So . . .' Paps stuck a toothpick between his lips. 'It's been a while.'

'A few weeks.'

'I think so. When did we last speak?' Paps cocked his head, as though trying to recall. 'Ah, yes. You collected your payment after that job. Excellent workmanship! The client was very pleased. As ever.' He folded his arms. 'My son tells me you are not long for this world.'

Kai smiled at the choice of phrase. 'I plan to leave. Yes.'

'You're not intending to go the way of the *martyrs*?'

Kai chuckled. Young freedom fighters who sacrificed their lives for the cause referred to themselves by this name. 'You know me better than that, Paps.'

'I thought so. But what you plan is still suicide – you realize that?'

Kai shrugged.

'Many have lost their lives to the sea over the years. Your own mother was one. But few have been rash enough to deliberately swim in those waters. And none that have done so survived. You are smarter than most.' Paps shook his head. 'In those shark-infested waters, there is *no* chance of survival. None!'

'I agree,' said Kai. 'Which is why I intend to go off the west side. Didn't Clod tell you?'

'Such a joker!' Paps laughed and patted Kai's shoulder. 'Into *Medusa*!?'

Kai nodded. Clod had kept his word and remained silent about the storm wave. Good. 'Colder and much more turbulent water. Fewer sharks. I have studied Medusa. She waxes and wanes with the tides. I believe, under the right conditions, it may be possible to slip round her. There's only one way to find out.'

'Instant death!' Paps laughed harder. 'She has swallowed whole fishing boats, cargo ships and even the occasional Nebulese naval vessel. You are clearly insane!'

Kai shrugged again.

'Even if you did manage it, you would then have acres of ocean to cross.' Paps's hand mimicked snapping jaws. 'And predators to keep at bay.'

'That little problem's been troubling me.' Kai leant over towards Paps. 'I thought you, with your connections, might be able to help.'

'Not even my influence spreads as wide as the ocean.'

Kai smiled. 'I need a gun.'

'A gun?' Paps's brow knitted. Glancing round to make sure they could not be overheard, he leant across the table.

61

'Of course my connections in *that* field are excellent. What exactly were you after?'

'I bought myself a pistol that could fire underwater,' said Kai.

'I think I've seen the sort of thing you mean,' said Paps. 'Clumsy, single-shot pieces, used by divers?'

Kai nodded.

'Not terribly effective,' said Paps.

'And in my case – totally useless,' said Kai. 'This one went off before I was ready. The great white was not impressed. I'm lucky to be here. Ended up dropping the thing.' He scratched his head. 'I suppose I could always go down and retrieve it. But then . . .'

'What use is a defective gun?'

'Exactly.'

Paps laughed. 'You could always try asking for your money back!'

'And buy myself a replacement?' said Kai. 'Unfortunately, there seems to have been a run on that particular type of weapon. No one has any to sell.'

Removing the toothpick from between his teeth, Paps examined it.

Kai watched him. 'I've got a better idea. You've got a job you want me for. Maybe we could negotiate something?'

'What – you work for me, and in return I find you some kind of underwater firearm?'

'Not just any kind. I don't want another of those useless, clapped-out, single-shot pieces.'

'You don't?' Paps squirmed uncomfortably. 'It's only a small job I have for you. What did you have in mind?'

'A *kombatordnantz XK7*. I saw a picture once. Nebulese special forces weapon. The handgun of choice.'

'Light years ahead of the antiquated junk we get round

here,' Paps said. 'But extremely hard to get hold of. Still if you do this little job for me, maybe I could lay my hands on one. They fire underwater. And no need to reload.'

Kai fidgeted. 'What do you want me to do?'

Paps scratched his nose. 'Collect something. In and straight out. Bring it back here.'

'Just a pick-up job!' This was unexpected.

'Something very, very valuable.'

What could be so important that Paps would choose him as courier? 'What's in the package?'

'I can't tell you.'

'Drugs?'

Paps shook his head. 'Something far more precious.'

Suddenly, in the piazza below, heads twisted as staccato bursts of gunfire floated across the town. Under the death rattle came a familiar bass throb, the dreaded sound – helicopter gunships.

Kai cocked his head. 'Sounds like harbourside.'

The roar of a missile was followed by an earsplitting explosion. Inside the restaurant and out, people had instinctively ducked, flinched and covered their heads. Some were under tables.

'Bloody reprisals.' Paps clenched his fists. 'A *martyr* got to the NebTech building a couple of days ago. Only killed herself. But broke plenty of glass.'

Down in the square a baby was crying. Slowly, trade and discourse resumed with the crack-crack and rattle of gunfire continuing in the distance.

'So what about this package?' said Paps. 'Will you collect it for me?'

'I deliver it, and you get me the *kombatordnantz*?'

Paps nodded. 'Depending on availability and how much it costs. You might have to do me another job for an *XK7*.'

'For an *XK7* it might be worth it.'

'I need it collecting as soon as possible,' said Paps. 'How about tonight?'

Kai shrugged. 'I had nothing planned.'

Paps offered his hand across the table. 'Then we have a deal?'

Kai shook the hand and nodded.

'One G-G-Green Star special!' Clod appeared, clutching a tray.

'With extra firebeans?' prompted Paps.

Clod nodded. 'Extra *extra* f-f-firebeans!' Placing a tankard and a large dish of meatballs, noodles and beans in front of Kai, he plonked down on the bench next to him. As Kai dug in, eating with his fingers, greedily slurping the food from its hot spicy sauce, Clod glanced across the table. His father was smiling.

13

Slick

Kai glanced left as he crossed the top of the road. The warehouse Paps had described to him sat squarely half-way down, sandwiched between a chandlery and one of the windowless, three-storey sweatshops that dotted the area. Cosy light shone out through cracks around a small door at the front of the warehouse. It was slightly ajar. Someone was working late. All as it should be.

But Kai kept on walking. Call it sixth sense. Call it whatever. He'd had an uneasy feeling about the job since the moment Paps had broached it. Paps only wanted him to collect, nothing more. It just didn't square. Paps could have used any one of a dozen other kids who worked for him. He could even have sent Clod. It wasn't as if Paps had provided a firearm for protection on this job. It was a straightforward pick-up, apparently, yet something so valuable only he, Kai, could be trusted to bring it home. But he didn't need a gun? It did not add up.

Kai walked past the chandlery and carried on along the road until, several minutes later, he reached the next side street. This one was all in darkness. No street lights, no light from the buildings. Ideal.

As he stepped into the shadows, a light rain was starting. Downtown could be hot as hell during the day, but there was often rain at night. Something to do with moist air cooling or some such. All he knew was rain and darkness suited him well. It seemed to intensify his awareness. He worked best on wet nights.

His eyes were quick to adjust to the absence of street lighting. His skin felt alive to the air. His listening felt tuned razor sharp to the slightest of sounds.

He stopped in front of a wreck of a building. Once a warehouse, stars now twinkled through holes in its roof. The big roller shutter door had long since fallen away. There had been some attempt to shore up the front with corrugated iron, but even that had seen better days.

Finding a place where the metal had been peeled back, Kai crouched, poked his head inside, and silently sniffed the air. Hints of human and animal urine, overwhelmed by the sour smell of decay. Rainwater drip-drip-dripped from the rotten roof, but there were no sounds to alert him. Treading warily, he made his way across the precarious rubble-strewn floor.

The back of the building had fallen away completely. Twisted rusted steel and huge chunks of masonry lay in piles the size of small mountains. Scrambling between them, Kai found himself in front of an enormous brick wall.

'What you got for me, Delta One? Over.' Mendel pressed the receive button on his walkie-talkie.

A blast of white noise echoed round the warehouse. *'Still quiet out here, chief. Nothing doing. De nada.'* The distorted voice carried across the silence. *'You want I should come in? Over.'*

'Stay put for now, Delta One. We sit this one out till the bitter end. Over.'

'Wilco, chief. Over and out.'

'Doesn't look as if our little friend is going to show.' The voice came from shadows to Mendel's left.

Mendel glanced at his watch. 'If he's coming, he's certainly cutting it fine.'

'What happens if he doesn't, chief?' The nasally voice drifted from further back behind one of the rows of crates stacked four high and running along the entire length of the warehouse.

'We still vacate as planned. At O two hundred. But after that . . .' Mendel scratched the side of his head. His eyebrows shifted skywards. 'We try again, I guess. We *need* this monkey.'

There was a small windowed office near the door entrance to the warehouse. A big figure of a man emerged from inside, crouched and pressed his cheek against brickwork near the door. He peered through a slim crack out into the street. 'It's like a ghost town. Not a soul.'

'Boss . . .' This voice came from deeper back in the warehouse. 'I'm getting cramp in my foot. I'm gonna take a stretch for a couple of minutes.'

'OK. But keep it silent and make sure you stay back in the shadows where no one can see you.' Getting up from the crate he'd been sitting on, Mendel took a stroll towards the door. 'I still have a good feeling about this one. My money says the kid won't let us down.'

Opening the skylight had been tricky, but nothing long deft fingers couldn't manage. Silence was the thing though. To do it and do it without making the slightest sound. Kai was confident he had carried it off.

Slowly he slid his way down a supporting strut that connected the roof to the side wall. From this lofty viewpoint he could see and hear everything. The whole warehouse was laid out below, the slightest sound travelled up to his ears. Perfect.

His caution, it appeared, had been well judged. Down amongst the crates and boxes a heavily armed reception party awaited his arrival. Six of them, as far as he could make out. Five men and one woman. And, as if that wasn't alarming enough, they had *Neb* accents. So much for this being a simple case of 'in and straight out'. The sensible thing to do would be to shin back up to the roof and head home. Or maybe go directly to the Green Star Noodle Bar and have it out with Paps.

But sensible was not his middle name. Paps would have to take his turn. Six Neb Secret Service agents had been waiting patiently to meet him. Having come this far, it would be a shame to disappoint them.

'Hey, Charlie, that you moving round?'

'Uh-uh. Not me. I'm sitting here still as a stone. Thought it was you.'

Mendel peered into the gloom. 'What's going on back there? You two getting twitchy?'

'I reckon we got rats, boss.'

'Big old warehouse this size,' said Mendel, 'bound to have.'

The two invisible men chuckled.

Leaving his position in front of the door, Mendel took a wander towards the aisles. 'Hang on in there, guys. He's coming. I can feel it.' He lowered his voice to a whisper. 'We've waited all this time. Let's not go blowing it now on the final stretch.'

'Okeedoke, chief.'

'Delta One,' Mendel spoke softly into the walkie-talkie. 'You got anything for me? Status report. Over.'

'*Soaked, chief. Getting wetter by the minute. Street's empty. I'll be glad when this is over. Over.*'

Chuckling echoed round the warehouse.

'Not long now, Delta One. Stay sharp for me. This thing is going down, I can feel it. I want you to keep those eyeballs peeled. Got that? Over.'

'*Roger, chief. Over and out.*'

The figure in front of Kai was kneeling with his back to him, crouched behind a crate. Using the crate top for support, he aimed his rifle down towards the front of the warehouse, peering through the telescopic laser sight. A hand gun hung loose in the shoulder holster at his right breast.

Kai held his breath the whole way. Extended between fingers and thumb he held one of the bolts he had removed from the skylight. Creeping up silently behind the crouching figure, he leant close, till his lips were just inches from the man's ear. At the exact moment he pressed the cold steel bolt against the man's neck, he spoke. '*Feel that?*' The lightest of whispers.

A nod.

'*Know what it is?*' he hissed.

'A gun?'

'*Correct. Move, and you're dead.*'

The crouching man turned to stone.

'Easy now . . .' In one slick movement, Kai snatched the automatic from the man's holster. 'That was painless.' The weapon was a Neb forces standard issue R14, fourteen rounds in the magazine. 'Now . . . very gently and very slowly,' he whispered, 'lay the nice shiny rifle down on the crate.'

Shaking slightly, the man obeyed.

'Good boy.' Kai pressed upwards with the bolt. 'OK. We're getting to our feet.' His voice was still a whisper. 'Keep the movements nice and slow.'

As the man got to his feet and gradually rose up to full height, Kai was forced to extend his bolt-holding arm. These Nebs were tall.

'Hey, Charlie!' It was the boss's voice. 'You muttering to yourself back there? What's up? Losing the plot?'

'Tell him you've got to stretch your legs.' Kai pressed the barrel of the man's automatic into his back. '*Be cool!*'

Making his way between the aisles, Mendel reached to the concealed holster that hugged his lower spine. A touch of his *kombatordnantz XK7* for reassurance. 'Charlie?'

'Sorry, chief.' The voice came out of the shadows. 'It's my er . . . my damn foot. All this kneeling. I think I'm getting cramp now too.'

'Go on then, Charlie.' Mendel headed back towards the door. 'Take a stretch. Just keep it quiet and make it brief.' His eye was drawn to the floor, to a sprinkle of dark spots on the concrete. He squatted to touch. *Wet.* Where had that come from? The skylight, ten metres above? It had been raining for some time. If the skylight was cracked or holed, why just the few spots of rain?

'Chief?'

Mendel turned.

Charlie looked sick. Someone was holding a gun to his head.

Reaching back, Mendel groped for the *XK7*.

'DON'T!' It was a boy's voice. 'Don't even THINK about it!!'

14

kombatordnantz

Kai gave Charlie a gentle push towards his boss. The nose of the gun was pressed hard against his skull, at the base, just behind the ear. 'One false move from you or your clowns, chief, and the brains of Agent Charlie here get splattered.'

'OK. Don't do anything hasty.'

'Put your hands UP.' Kai inched Charlie forwards. 'WHERE I CAN SEE THEM!!' Shouting worked. 'That's better. Now, what's your name, mister boss man?'

'Mendel.'

'All right, Mendel. Turn away!' Kai shoved Charlie hard. 'Keep walking, Charlie, till you hit the wall at the front of the warehouse.'

'OK.' Charlie walked.

Lifting the back of Mendel's jacket, Kai removed the gun he'd seen him reach for. 'Hey! An *XK7*!' The legendary top-spec piece, the one he had asked for from Paps. Fancy that! It was the first time he had actually seen one. 'Nice!' He clicked off the safety, pressed the laser-sight button and aimed the red beam at the back of Charlie's head. 'Any other little toys you want to tell me about, Mendel?'

'That's it.' Mendel sounded weary, resigned. 'Just the *XK7*.'

'Let's check.' Sticking Charlie's automatic in his belt,

Kai patted down Mendel with his free hand. 'I want all your agents to lay down their guns.' He spoke nice and loud so the whole warehouse could hear him. 'I want them to step out of their hiding places and put their hands on their heads.'

Mendel nodded and obeyed. 'You heard what the kid said, guys. No complications. Just do it.'

'Thank you.' Kai kept it loud. 'Now, one by one, Mister Mendel here is going to call out your names. Then, one by one, unarmed and with your hands in the air where I can see them, you are going to make your way down to the front of the warehouse. Agent Charlie is standing with his nose pressed against the wall. I want each of you to do the same. Any deviation from these instructions and I will shoot your boss and shoot you.' He prodded Mendel. 'OK, boss man. The names. Start with the guy in the office.'

As Mendel called the names and the agents made their way forwards, Kai manoeuvred his hostage towards the door. With Charlie's gun now jabbed in Mendel's kidneys, Kai kept the red eye of the *XK7* tracking the progress of each agent. 'Nice and smooth. That's it. Noses against the brickwork.' He prodded Mendel. 'While we're at it, what about poor old wetboy? Get on the walkie-talkie. Let's bring him in too.'

Mendel nodded. 'Delta One, make your way back to the warehouse. Over.' He held the walkie-talkie at arm's length so Kai could hear.

'*Thought you were never going to ask, chief. I'm coming in. Over.*'

'For your sake,' said Kai, 'I hope none of that was coded. Any funny business and . . .'

'Trust me.'

'Oh yeah.' Kai chuckled. 'Trust you – that's funny!' He pushed Mendel behind the door. 'OK. Now *shhhh*.'

The door opened. 'Am I wet or am I . . .' The rain-sodden agent froze as he spotted his colleagues lined up with their noses against the wall.

'Welcome to the party!' Kai stepped out from behind the door, using Mendel as a shield. 'Please remove any weapons you may be carrying, lay them on the ground, then join your colleagues who, as you can see, are sniffing the brickwork. Sorry – we're out of towels.'

Soggy Delta One complied.

'Wonderful!' Shutting and locking the door, Kai nudged Mendel towards the crates he had earlier been sitting on. 'This is all rather cosy. Nobody we've left out?'

'No.'

'Excellent!' Kai gestured. 'If you'd like to sit down and make yourself comfortable, I think it's time we had a chat.'

Man and boy sat studying one another in silence.

Quiet and motionless, Kai became aware of his galloping heartbeat. Whose was running fastest, he wondered, his or this Mendel's? The man looked calm, considering he had a gun pointing at him. Perhaps he was used to it. They probably got trained for that kind of thing.

Mendel's eyes followed Kai's every movement, as he swapped the *XK7* from right hand to left, wiped the palm of his right hand on his leg, then swapped the gun back again. 'You're probably wondering who we are. And why we were armed and waiting in this warehouse?'

'Just a little curious.' For a moment Kai felt panic hovering. What had he walked into? How seriously out of his depth was he here? 'I was hired to pick up a package.'

'There is no package.' Mendel's voice was a low

monotone. Calm. Flat even. 'Sorry. We duped your friend. I can see how our little reception committee might appear a touch aggressive. But there's a simple explanation.'

'And I am dying to hear it.'

'We are Nebulese.'

Kai's grip tightened on the *XK7*. 'You don't say.'

'The weapons were for defensive purposes only.'

'Don't tell me – you're from the Ministry of Arts? Here to arrange a visit by the national dance company?'

'Alas, no.' Mendel offered a conciliatory smile. 'I'm head of SIA. The Security and Intelligence Agency. I'm here because I wanted to talk to you.'

Kai narrowed his eyes. 'Me? Me *personally*?' He wiped his palm again.

Mendel nodded. 'The agents were here simply for my protection.' He started to lean forwards, then seemed to remember the situation. There was still a gun pointing at him. He changed his mind and sat back again. 'For me to come here is extremely dangerous.'

'You're lucky you're not dead already,' said Kai. 'You need better agents.' He fiddled with the *XK7*. Let Mendel sweat. 'We don't know each other. We have no connection. So, why me? What exactly did you want to talk about?'

'Leaving Portobello.'

Kai eyed him suspiciously. Did they know about his plans? 'It's not actually illegal.'

'No,' said Mendel. 'It's not. Our government tries to . . . *discourage* it.'

'And why is that?'

Mendel's eyes searched Kai's for clues – how best to respond. 'Portobello is a useful pool of cheap labour.'

The unexpectedly honest answer unnerved Kai. What was Mendel's game? 'No one ever leaves,' he said.

Mendel nodded. 'But I've come to offer you a way out.' The slight smile again. 'I'm here to offer you Nebulese citizenship.'

The *kombatordnantz XK7* was suddenly right in Mendel's face. The red laser dot bang in the middle of his forehead. 'Very funny!' Kai gripped the gun with both hands. 'What were you expecting? That I'd keel over with shock?' His hands were shaking. 'Was that the plan? Grab the gun?'

'No.'

'You must think I'm stupid! Is that what Paps told you?'

'No.'

'Nebula doesn't offer citizenship to Portobellans. Not even to their collaborators.'

'This is different.' Sweat was beading on Mendel's brow. 'My government has a problem of such potentially catastrophic proportions, it is prepared to make such an offer.'

'To *me*? Why would they do that? I'm a nobody. What possible use could I be?' Kai felt flutters of panic. 'This does not make sense.' He steadied his grip on the *XK7*. '*Explain.*'

Mendel took a deep breath. 'Two young people from our country have crossed the border into Portobello. We want you to track them down.'

Kai searched Mendel's face for signs of deception. This man knew about the kind of work he had done. Paps must have told him. 'I never heard of Nebulese taking refuge in Portobello before. How young?'

'Around your age.'

'My age!' They had to be total desperadoes. 'Portobello is a tough city. Nebulese kids wouldn't stand a chance here. What did they do? Kill somebody?'

'I suppose you could say they stole something.' Mendel shrugged. 'It's not so much what they did, as what they *are*.'

'I don't understand.'

'I'm sure even here it must be common knowledge that Nebula runs research programmes into human genetic enhancement.'

Kai nodded. 'The Super Race.'

'We now have a whole generation walking around our streets who are moderately enhanced.'

'The world's fittest, healthiest and most beautiful nation,' quoted Kai. He had read that, or heard it somewhere.

'Whatever,' said Mendel. 'Recent trends in climate change and rising sea levels have caused all sorts of problems inland with flooding. This region has also, as you must know, been dogged by an increase in tsunami activity.'

'What we call storm waves.'

Mendel nodded. 'Our scientists have turned their attention to new kinds of genetic enhancement. Over the last few decades they've been working on a second generation, better adapted to surviving in water.'

'In case the flooding and storm waves get worse?'

'Oh, they will. The scientists are certain.'

'Then that's real smart thinking.' Kai lowered the gun. For such a sophisticated weapon, the *XK7* still felt heavy after so long.

Mendel nodded. 'That's what the two fugitives have stolen.'

'Their own genes? They're genetically enhanced?'

'Yes. They were part of the research programme. If they escape beyond Portobello into the wider world, decades of work will potentially be made worthless.'

76

'How come?'

'They can pass on their modified genes.'

'You mean if they have children?'

Mendel nodded. 'It's hard to convey just how much is at stake.' His face was grave. 'Our president will *stop at nothing* to prevent such an outcome.'

Kai held Mendel's bleak gaze. 'Then why pick me?'

'You are the best there is . . .' said Mendel, '. . . apparently. You know the coastline better than anyone in Portobello. You also know the streets and people of Downtown.'

'True enough.'

'You are fit. You are cunning and tricky, as you proved tonight. And you are still a child.'

A child. Kai smiled to himself. It was a while since he'd been called that, except in provocation. Nebulese and Portobellan ideas of childhood were a little different.

'You are an expert at finding and following people,' said Mendel. 'You are not averse to breaking the law and have even, on occasion, I understand, carried out assassinations. You have no allegiances. You are your own master. And most importantly, our mutual friend says you can be trusted.'

'And you believe him!' Kai snorted. 'That man is easily Downtown's biggest blackguard. There's no one more devious.' He got to his feet, shaking his head. 'For someone in charge of such a powerful organization, you show very poor judgement.' He headed for the door. 'That bothers me.'

'You are our best hope.' Mendel hurried after him.

Kai kept walking, past the agents with their noses against the brickwork.

'And we are yours,' said Mendel. 'By a long stretch.'

Kai halted by the door. The alternative was shark-infested waters and a whirlpool. He glanced at Mendel. 'I've no reason on this earth to trust you.'

'Do you trust your current employer?' said Mendel.

Kai scowled.

'Clearly not,' said Mendel. 'And you never have. But there was enough reciprocal need for you both to work together. So you did.'

Kai grimaced. 'Never again.'

Mendel shrugged. 'What have you got to lose by working for us?' The eyes twinkled. 'You've everything to gain.'

'A ticket out of this dump?' Kai opened the door. In spite of who Mendel was, there was something about him he warmed to. 'I'll think about it.'

'Don't take too long.' Unbuckling his holster, Mendel held it out to Kai. 'We have a ticking clock. Just five days to come up with the goods. After that the offer expires.'

'And then?'

In the half light all the colour seemed to have drained from Mendel's face. His expression was grave. 'So does Portobello.'

15

Windswept and Desolate

Kai took the small flight of steps two at a time, his pace synchronized to the beat of his own blood pumping. It was loud and getting louder with every step he took towards the object of his anger.

Paps was propped against the bar, reading a paper. He looked up and smiled. 'Good morning!' He glanced at his timepiece. 'Or should I say good afternoon? Did we have a late night?'

Knowing the falseness of this jocularity, Kai smiled back.

'The courier returns!'

'He does.'

'And does he have something for me?'

'He does.' Swinging his fist hard and fast, Kai sank it into Paps's fat belly.

'*Oooof!*' Paps gasped and doubled over.

'You set me up!' There was rage in Kai's voice. 'You *betrayed me!*'

Struggling for breath, Paps slowly straightened up. A couple of concerned customers had scrambled to their feet. A waiter appeared at the bottom of the steps, Clod hovered close by. Paps dismissed their concern with a wave. Breathing hard, he scowled at Kai and clutched the counter for support. 'Quite a punch!'

'That's all you've got to say for yourself?' Kai's fists were still clenched.

Paps gave a deep, beseeching shrug. 'What could I do?' His gaze flitted around the room, settling on Clod. 'They threatened to hurt my child.'

Kai's glare was pure cold scorn. 'Now why don't I believe you?'

'Honestly!' Paps gestured, 'He's all I have!'

'And more than you deserve,' said Kai. 'You're a greedy, lying, cheating, bullying scumbag!' And turning on his heel, he marched out.

Sky the colour of slate. And air cooler than it had been for days. A gale was blowing up. The sea was big and getting bigger. As waves broke on the shore they made that satisfying booming sound, fat and muffled as though someone were detonating dynamite deep beneath the sand.

The beach was windswept and desolate. Kai was glad, he preferred it like that. Preferred it empty. He had been coming here as long as he could remember. Always drawn to the sea.

The lifeguard cabin was essentially a hut on stilts. At its base sat a large wooden crate. It was here that the lifeguards stored the bulk of their equipment – their ropes, floats, surfboards, canoes and so on. At an early age Kai had taken to picking the padlock and 'borrowing' the surfboards when the lifeguards were off duty. Now he crouched down beside the crate to take shelter from the wind.

With a quick glance round to check he was not being watched, he slipped the *kombatordnantz XK7* out from its holster under his shirt and placed it on the sand. Was this the 'something' that he needed before he could escape?

Covering the gun with his hooded top, he lay back against the crate and tried to push the foolish words of a blind old woman from his mind.

His gaze stretched out over the faded blue-grey sea to the faint horizon, where ocean and sky became one. Mistrusting the weather, Portobello's fishermen had earlier returned to the harbour. But somewhere out there, Nebulese navy ships would still be patrolling.

He closed his eyes to let his imagination travel further. Not so very far beyond that horizon, indeed probably under the very same overcast sky, scores of tiny islands lay sprinkled on the ocean. Could he really, with the help of the storm wave, travel that far . . .?

'I knew I'd find you s-s-somewhere by the sea.'

Kai blinked open his eyes. Clod. 'If you're here with a message from your father, I'd think twice before delivering it.'

Clod shook his head. 'He doesn't know I'm h-h-here. I wanted to f-f-find out what happened.'

'What happened?' Kai's laugh was brittle. 'I made the mistake of coming back to Downtown, that's what happened.'

Clod sat down beside him, out of the wind.

'Then I made the mistake of listening to the blind prophetess,' said Kai.

'M-M-Mushirah?' Clod gave a nervous chuckle. 'You've n-n-never believed in all th-th-that nonsense!'

'Thank you for reminding me.' Kai sighed wearily. 'But she had seemed to know things . . . After which, I foolishly agreed to do one last job for your father. Turns out he sent me into a trap – a little meeting with the SIA.'

81

'*What?*'

Kai nodded. 'Nebulese secret agents. I caught them off guard though.'

Clod looked around anxiously. 'Do they w-w-want you to *sp-sp-spy?*'

'No. They want me to hunt down two Nebulese fugitives.'

Clod's mouth gaped.

'Kids. Our age, near enough. They escaped from one of the laboratories where they do their genetic research.'

'So the stories are tr-tr-true?'

Kai shrugged. 'Sounds that way. The SIA believe they're hiding here, somewhere in Portobello.'

'You can sn-sn-sniff them out, if anyone can. Wh-wh-what are the SIA offering?'

'A ticket out of here. Nebulese passport.'

Clod's eyes widened. '*What!?*'

'I said I'd think about it.'

'You're so c-c-cool!'

Kai snorted. 'I didn't know what to say. The whole thing was so unexpected, it completely threw me.' He scooped up a handful of sand. 'Working for the Nebs doesn't bother me. It's a job like any other.'

'But b-b-best that no one in Downtown f-f-finds out.'

'Of course.' He let the sand trickle out through his fingers. 'Now I've had time to mull it over, it's not such a bad situation to be in. If I find these two fugitives – all well and good. If I don't, I can just go ahead with my original plan.'

'Catch the w-w-wave?'

Kai nodded. 'Oh, I nearly forgot . . .' Slipping the *kombatordnantz XK7* from under his hoodie, he dropped it in Clod's lap. 'Look what I found!'

Clod gasped and flinched, like he thought the gun might explode.

'You know what it is?' said Kai.

Clod nodded.

'I thought I might try it out,' said Kai. 'See if it shoots underwater, like your father said.'

16

Something Lurking

A long line of buoys marked the submerged wall of netting that kept underwater predators away from the beach. Kai rose and fell as he ploughed through the choppy sea. The buoys rose and fell too. Appearing and disappearing.

Just a short distance away, the orange sphere Kai had been aiming for suddenly bobbed into view. He felt a surprising surge of relief. The waves were bigger than he had judged from the shore; the rip current had been stronger than he'd felt it in a long time. For a while he had struggled to escape its pull and stay on course. A short rest before he turned around would be welcome.

The buoy was large, smooth and wet, so even in a calm sea there was nothing to grab hold of. Chains tethered the net to the buoy and the buoy to the ocean bed. Under less boisterous conditions, Kai would have braced his feet against them. Not today. With the huge rise and fall of the ocean, the entire buoy was being dragged under the surface every time a wave rolled by.

Treading water, Kai turned towards the shore. Light had faded early. It was raining. The sky was so thickly clouded it was hard to guess where the sun had set. Nebula's slopes shimmered with lights but there were few yet twinkling down in Portobello. On the shore line he could just make out a huddled figure beneath the lifeguards' cabin, silhouetted against the sand and the bleached crate. Kicking hard for extra lift, Kai raised an arm and waved. The figure waved back.

Kai shivered. From out of nowhere he had the uneasy sense there was something behind him. That he was being *watched*. Always his instinct came alive in the sea. Became louder. Still treading water, he twizzled around. Nothing. Just smoky sky and dark glossy ocean. Wisps of white.

He hadn't swum out here just to test the gun. Something else had been driving him. Hunter instinct. Thinking like the prey. What were they like? Where would they go? What would they do? That part of his mind had kicked into action, as if he'd already decided to take the job.

The twitchy feeling was strong. He was on the frontier, there could be sharks nearby. Time to dive. Taking a deep breath, he kicked hard, sculling to raise himself above the swell. Then jack-knifed below the surface.

Hearing altered underwater. The background clutter of sounds got stifled, dampened out. And the body's internal noises grew louder. The tiniest gurgle became a loud event. All movement generated sound. Kai swam down, pulling and kicking, strong and wide. Down, close against the net.

The water was dark now, and here there was sand churned up by the rollers. He couldn't see far but straight away the poor state of the nets was clear. There were holes. Holes where two or three squares together had been ripped and torn. Holes he could get not just his hand, but his whole head through. A small shark would have no problem.

Small sharks weren't the danger.

Kai swam further down, following the course of the nets. The more he saw the more he was shocked. The nets were disintegrating. A storm was coming, and with it a rough

85

sea. The nets would be in shreds before long. Then there would be nothing to protect swimmers. Though if this was the storm wave coming, torn nets would be the least of Downtown's problems.

Instinct said this was too soon for the storm wave. That other part of his mind said so too. From what he could remember, the groaning sounds from the ocean were still too few and far between. Too short in duration. When a mother gave birth, the groans she made got faster, closer together and louder when something was on the way. That's how he remembered it being with the wave.

The uneasy sensation hadn't faded. He had pushed it to the back, but now it was clamouring. He *was* being watched. The *XK7* was in the holster at his belt. Maybe now it would have a target. Maybe now he'd need it.

He jerked round, alerted by something at the corner of his vision. Though he moved fast, it had gone. But his heart was thumping. He had the weirdest feeling. What could he have glimpsed so fleetingly? It had looked like . . . no. He pushed the idea from his mind. A face? At this depth? It couldn't possibly have been.

The dim light could play tricks on perception. But something was out there, skirting round him, just beyond the limits of his vision. What was that? A flick of fin? A twitch of tail? Something he recognized. *What was it?*

His gut tightened. His body flexed. Taking the *XK7*, he clicked off the safety and stretched it out at arm's length, linking his two hands. A gentle porpoise kick rippled down his body to his feet. Slowly at first, then building speed. Soon it was one powerful, muscular whipping action. His senses were alert. The chase was on!

There it was! Over to the right.

Vanished.

And again, to the left.

Vanished again.

Now down below him.

Kai surged.

Then again – off to the side.

Fast though Kai was, he wasn't able to gain on the creature long enough to catch more than tantalizing glimpses. But with each one he became more certain it was not the familiar enemy. This wasn't a shark.

What had got through the nets? Was it toying with him?

Dizziness was beginning. He needed air. And there it was again! The tail of the thing. Just ahead of him, just out of vision, streaking in towards the shore. Suddenly he had the feeling he was chasing himself, catching up on his own tail. It was *two feet*. Two legs pressed together, undulating in a perfect, powerful, wavelike motion.

'*Paaaaagh!*' Breaking the surface, Kai gasped for breath. '*Heeeeeugh!*' His heart jumped like it might any second leap from his chest. His lungs flapped like trapped birds.

He had lost it. Whatever he had seen down there, it had got away.

The thick carpet of cloud was breaking up. Strong winds drove silhouettes scudding across the early stars.

'I know the rain has st-st-stopped,' Clod shivered. 'But it's n-n-night n-now and g-getting *very* c-c-cold.'

Kai remained motionless, staring out at the dark sea.

'And that was my t-t-teeth ch-ch-chattering, not my st-stutter,' added Clod. 'Come on, K-K-Kai. What's the p-p-point?'

'Go home if you want to,' said Kai. 'I'm watching.'

'W-w-watching for what? You can't see anything in this l-l-light!'

Kai hurled a handful of sand at the wind. His instinct had brought him here at this time to this beach. He had gone out into the sea intending to test the *XK7*, but not fired a shot. He had seen *something*. But what had it been?

'I don't know what you s-s-saw,' said Clod 'But wh-wh-whatever it was, it didn't w-walk into the sea. B-b-believe me.'

It had to have done. It'd had *feet*. It had swum like a fish, but it had definitely had feet. And hadn't he thought he'd seen a face? Boy or girl, he couldn't say. One of the fugitives? Mendel had said they were 'better adapted' to surviving in water. But that deep? Swimming like that? Who else could it have been? Had instinct brought him close to his prey this quickly? It had happened before. He was hunting already, without realizing it. 'You're certain?'

'I was s-sitting here the whole t-t-time,' said Clod. 'The beach was eh . . . eh . . . eh . . . *eegh*!' He bit his knuckle, frustrated.

'Empty?'

Clod gave a weary nod.

'What's the first thing fugitives would do?' said Kai. 'Check obvious escape routes, right?'

'I sup-p-pose.'

It made sense. It had to have been them. 'What other priorities might they have?' He was at it again, thinking like the prey he was stalking. 'Somewhere to hide. And then what?'

Clod shrugged. 'G-g-get armed, maybe?'

Kai nodded. 'If they aren't already.'

Using the crate for support, Clod struggled, grunting, to his feet. 'C-c-come on, Kai. Who knows wh-wh-what it was? You were underw-w-water an awful l-l-long time.'

It was true, he had been. He was tired. He needed rest.

The last twenty-four hours had been tough, and maybe his judgement was off. 'You think I was imagining things?'

Clod scowled and shivered. 'I'm t-t-too cold to c-c-care!'

Getting to his feet, Kai put on his hoodie. He had not taken his eyes off the sea since he got out. Whatever it was he'd seen in the water, one thing was certain – he, she or it was still out there somewhere.

As another dark wave rolled over the buoy to gather speed and crash down hard on the beach, two heads bobbed, one on either side. Teeth chattering, too cold and numb to speak, their eyes watched the figures on the beach.

At last. The boys were moving. One with a limp. And the other one, the one who had been searching in the water with a gun. The two of them were leaving.

Now they could swim to shore.

17

Phoebe and Phoenix

With her hood clenched tight around her face, and Phoenix's jacket wrapped round her for extra warmth, Phoebe lay curled between two large angular blocks of concrete. Not exactly luxurious. But her teeth were chattering and she couldn't stop shivering anyway, so what did she care about comfort? Here, below the high-tide line, on the ocean side of the harbour wall, everything was covered in tiny barnacle shells. Snugness was out of the question.

The rain had let up. There was that to be thankful for. And it was very dark. She could be thankful for that too. Who would come out along the harbour wall on a night like this? Who would brave the driven wind and seaspray? Who would scramble down here amongst the concrete and seaweed? Only someone mad. Or a desperate fugitive. She had screamed with fright when a crab scuttled up her leg. But who would have heard? She clutched herself tighter. Here, down in the uncomfortable, damp dark, at least she was safe.

Ordinarily she loved to be in water or near it. Having only ever swum in pools and tanks, it was such a thrill, finally, to be in contact with the real, unenclosed sea. It had been teeming with myriad small creatures, vibrant with all manner of life. She had only ever read about it or seen images of a small part of what she had so far encountered.

But right now, with her body temperature falling so low, to be warm was all she wanted.

She shivered. Were she and Phoenix crazy to have done what they had done? To have left the cocooned life of safety and comfort. To go on the run. To be wet and freezing to death on the inhospitable edge of some inhospitable town. Alone.

Phoebe screwed her eyes shut but tears still came, trickling warmth down her cheeks. Sobs too, reaching up and shaking her from her core. Her breath came in shaky gasps. A sound, part howl, part cry, welled up from somewhere deeper than her lungs. She clamped a hand to her mouth.

What was it? Where was it coming from? It wasn't fear. It wasn't the cold. Oh, she recognized it now. Her familiar old friend from the still, small hours of early morning. Back in that airless, claustrophobic cell. A feeling she had known for as long as she could remember. The ache that used to wake her. The longing. *Loneliness.*

Was her old friend playing tricks on her? Had loneliness warped her perception? Still, when she closed her eyes, she saw the face. It could only have been the most fleeting of glimpses, and it had happened – if it had happened – at such dimly lit depths. But the extraordinary features were burned into her memory.

No doubt about it. The cold, the lack of light, the deep water, being in a new environment – all these could have distorted what she saw. What else could it have been? What could she have mistaken for a face? She knew the answer before she had asked the question. Nothing. It had been what she had seen. It had been a face down there. Quite distinct. The face of a boy.

That wasn't possible.

91

Gently she rocked herself. After having been in saltwater so long, her tears actually tasted sweet. Her sobs were subsiding. And now the shivering and teeth chattering had returned. The cold hadn't gone away, she had merely forgotten it, momentarily, for other misery.

It made her angry. Wasn't she supposed to have been *designed*? Wasn't she supposed to be new and improved? The vanguard of a genetically enhanced generation, better adapted to surviving in water? What was the use of the great advantages – being able to swim like a fish and stay submerged underwater for long periods without breathing, and all the other really useful things – if, after only a few hours in the ocean, she was shivering and dying from cold? But of course she was only a prototype. Right now she would like to confront her designer.

'*Pssst!*'

As Phoebe glanced up, a black shape sprang from the harbour wall. Jerking back in startled reflex, she cracked her head against a block. '*Ow!*'

Phoenix crouched beside her. 'Oh, you poor thing!' He cradled her head against his shoulder. 'You are *really* cold!' His long strong arms wrapped themselves around her and began to rub her back. 'I've found us the perfect hiding place.' He squeezed her close, rubbing warmth into her. 'We'll soon have you there. Soon have you cosy, safe and secure. Come on.'

No gates or customs post cordoned off the harbour area from the rest of Downtown. A small militia building overlooked the various wharves and the wide cobbled dockside, but the lights were off and the guards had gone home for the night. The only boats to tie up in this harbour were the vessels of the local fishing fleet.

As Phoenix and Phoebe made their way across the cobbles, boats rocked and strained against ropes. Burgees fluttered manically in the wind, cables pinged against masts. The big warehouses and most of the smaller sheds where the fishermen stored their gear were locked and silent, but the harbour was by no means deserted. People were coming to and fro. On the wharves, groups of fisherman sat smoking and drinking. They chatted and laughed as they mended their nets. On some of the boats, small jobs were being carried out and repairs being made.

Phoebe clutched Phoenix closer. She had not shaken off the shivers, but the walk had taken the edge off the cold and her teeth were no longer chattering. 'Where are we heading? It must be one of the warehouses. Is it?'

Phoenix smiled and made a zipping gesture across his lips.

'Oh, go on!' hissed Phoebe. 'Tell me!' She glanced around. They had passed most of the harbourside buildings and were heading towards the other arm of Portobello's harbour wall. Most of the wall lay in complete darkness apart from the lighthouse at its furthest end.

Phoenix nodded towards the final jetty, in the shadows at the edge of the illuminated area. Three fishing boats were moored to it. And not a person in sight. With a few furtive glances to make sure they were not being watched, the two of them dashed on to the jetty.

Phoenix beckoned Phoebe towards the smallest boat, bobbing up and down, alone at the far end. As he helped her on board, the boat lurched with the heave of the sea. Phoebe felt herself surrendering to exhaustion.

'In here.' Phoenix held open the low cabin door. 'There's six steps. And no room to move at the bottom. So lie on the bench and I'll follow you down.'

*

Phoebe opened her eyes. It was dark, very dark, but her eyes adapted easily to poor light. The air reeked of fish. She remembered; she was in the tiny, cramped cabin of the fishing boat. Looking up, the silhouette of Phoenix was just visible against the window of the cabin door. She smiled at him. He had lain down with her, to melt away her shivers with his warmth. He must have succeeded. She had drifted off.

'Feeling any better?' Phoenix descended to the bottom steps.

'Much,' said Phoebe. She sat up. 'Thanks. What you did was really sweet.'

'Got to look after each other, haven't we?'

Phoebe nodded. 'How long have I been asleep?'

'Not long,' said Phoenix. 'Couple of hours?'

'What have you been up to?'

'Keeping lookout,' said Phoenix. 'Thinking about our situation. What we do next. Where we go from here. Here!' He tossed a small package into Phoebe's lap. 'Portobellan chocolate. I found it up top. Not a patch on what we're used to. But . . .'

'Mmmm!' Phoebe had already taken a hungry bite. 'It's still chocolate!'

Phoenix nodded.

'So,' said Phoebe, getting to her feet, 'come up with any great ideas?'

Phoenix struck a match and used it to light a stub of candle on a saucer. The warm glow illuminated his sombre expression. 'I think we need to arm ourselves.'

'*What?*' Phoebe almost choked. If she hadn't been fully awake, she was now. She coughed and swallowed the chocolate. 'Why?'

'Because the boy you thought you saw in the water,'

94

said Phoenix, 'might have been carrying a gun.' Phoebe scowled.

'Not just that,' said Phoenix. 'Half the population are armed. The militia, the freedom fighters. Even everyday citizens – we've both seen them walking around with guns scarcely concealed beneath their cloaks and jackets. If they knew who we were, not one of them would hesitate to pull the trigger.'

'I don't like the idea of being armed,' said Phoebe. 'We never agreed to this when we were planning our escape.'

'It was never something we discussed!' snapped Phoenix.

'That doesn't mean we should just *do it!*'

Phoenix glared.

'OK . . .' Phoebe took a deep breath and sat back down. 'OK. We're both getting overexcited. Let's try to calm down and think about this logically.'

'OK,' Phoenix grunted.

'How would we get hold of weapons,' said Phoebe, 'just supposing we agreed to? Either by breaking in somewhere or by attacking someone. That means putting ourselves in unnecessary danger.'

'It's a trade-off,' said Phoenix. 'Once we have the weapons we can protect ourselves more effectively.'

'We're supposed to be smarter, stronger, faster. We have all sorts of advantages that these people don't have. Why do we need weapons?'

'Because *they* have weapons.' Phoenix was shouting again. 'Sooner or later it's going to be kill or be killed. And when that moment comes, I don't want to be staring down the barrel of a gun with nothing but my cunning and agility to save me.'

'I don't think I can kill somebody.'

'It's not so hard.'

'How would you know?'

'I've done it.'

'What?' Phoebe stared. Froze. 'What do you mean?'

Phoenix shook his head.

Phoebe was furious now. 'What are you talking about?'

'OK. I killed the fisherman who owns this boat.' Phoenix didn't blink.

'What!?' Phoebe's head spun. She couldn't take this in. 'Why are you saying this?'

'Because I did,' said Phoenix. 'You were freezing to death. We needed somewhere safe to hide. I spotted him alone on the wharf by his boat. No one else around.' As he leant forwards, the candlelight threw his eyes into deep shadow. 'I went over to speak to him.' He made a twisting gesture with his hands and a snapping sound in his throat.

Clutching herself, Phoebe shrank back against the wooden panelling. 'You *killed* him?' Her voice sounded broken.

Phoenix shrugged. 'I'd been looking high and low. Found nothing. Now we've got a safe little base. For a few days, at least.'

Phoebe's head was shaking, her mouth was moving but no sounds were coming out. 'I . . . I . . . I can't believe it!' She peered at him. 'What's happened to you? Are you *insane*!?'

Suddenly, Phoenix roared with laughter and reached out towards her.

'Don't *touch* me!' Phoebe jerked away.

But Phoenix moved fast. Jumping up, he grabbed her. '*Phoebe!*' A broad smile cracked his face. 'You believed me!'

'Get off me!' Phoebe kicked and struggled.

Phoenix had weight and strength on his side. He tightened his arms around her. 'Phoebe, listen to me. How am *I* going to kill someone, a fully grown man, with my own bare hands? *I don't have a weapon!*'

Phoebe's struggling subsided. She glared. 'Did you just put me through all that to make a point?' Her fists clenched. 'About getting guns?'

'Look . . .' Phoenix released her. 'We're not going to agree on this. Maybe we should just accept that. I'm going to find myself something to defend myself with.'

Phoebe slumped on the bench seat.

Crouching beside her, Phoenix stroked her cheek. 'If you don't want to stay with me once I'm armed, that's your decision. We can separate.' Getting to his feet, he made his way up the steps to the cabin door. 'I'm going out for a look around. I shouldn't be too long. You have a think about being on your own in this world.' He winked. 'Don't wait up.'

18

Burnt Out and Crashing

'Hey!' Kai swivelled and shook his fist at no one in particular. 'Look where you're going!'

Grabbing his elbow, Clod steered him out of people's way. 'Just p-p-pipe down and stop treading on toes. Or you're g-g-going to get us into t-trouble.'

'I'm fine,' Kai chuckled. 'It's them you want to have words with.' He felt good. Relaxed. His edges had softened. He had a smile in his heart. 'I was burnt out and crashing when I got to the bar. But now I'm *fine*.'

Clod shook his head disapprovingly. 'Drinking and blazing?'

Kai narrowed his eyes, hawked and spat into the gutter. He felt good. He had been enjoying himself down the Old Neptune bar, overlooking the beach. Unwinding in the company of fishermen and stevedores. They had been smoking rock through a water pipe. People called it 'blazing' because of the way the rock herb flamed up when the smoker sucked on the pipe.

Rock, water, fire and air. The ritual seemed to be as much a part of why they did it as the light, numbing buzz. Kai would never be tempted to drink or smoke, his wits were too important to him to risk dulling them. But he liked the warm company – the ritual, the jokes and the tales all relaxed him. The men from the harbour had the best stories without a doubt. 'Dragging me away at this unearthly hour!' Kai snarled. 'You'd better have a good reason.'

'You can d-d-decide for yourself,' chuckled Clod. 'We're there!'

Though it was the middle of the night, the narrow street they had entered was packed with people. Like most streets in Downtown this one had no lighting. What illumination there was came from the apartments. Residents were out on their balconies, chatting and looking down on the spectacle. Some held torches and lamps.

Down on the ground several flares were being held aloft in the middle of the crowd. Smoking and dribbling sparks, they burned against the darkness with a blinding white light.

The noisy, excited crowd strained to get closer, to hear and see more.

'What's this?' Kai scowled. 'You brought me to someone's wedding festivities?'

'It's n-n-no wedding.'

'OK then, birthday party?'

Clod shook his head. 'This is not a c-c-celebration at all.'

'Then why are we here?'

'I thought you m-m-might be curious. There's bccn a m-m-murder. Several in f-f-fact in one house.'

Kai scowled. 'There are murders most nights in Portobello. What's so special about these?'

'These were f-f-freedom fighters.'

Kai stared unsteadily. It was unheard of for a freedom fighter to be attacked. They were local heroes. Criminal gangs stayed away from them. And the rest of Downtown had a deep respect. His hazy mind was still sharp enough to grasp the significance. *They kept guns*. He looked again towards the flares. He could see now that they were militia standard issue. 'The militia investigating?'

Clod nodded. 'As we sp-sp-speak.'

'Let's try and get a closer look.'

Kai pushed through the crowd, ducking and barging. Bringing up the rear, Clod received the odd kick and punch from disgruntled Downtowners, venting their anger at having been shoved or had their toes trodden on.

A small section of the street had been entirely roped off. While men and women in militia uniforms held back the crowd, coopted onlookers held aloft the flares that lit the scene. In front of an ordinary-looking doorway, officers were crouched round three bodies. There were trails of blood from the doorway and more pooling round the corpses. The bodies had been carried or even dragged from the house and laid out on the ground for examination. Freshly dead.

Kai turned to the woman he had squeezed next to. 'What's the story?'

The woman peered at him disapprovingly. 'A young man, his wife and the man's brother. All murdered. But so far no sign of their daughter.'

'You know them?'

The woman nodded. 'We live just at the end of the street. They were in the Portobellan Freedom Fighters, the PFF. Everybody knew that. The biggest and best organized of the groups involved in armed struggle against the Nebulese. Everyone knew someone who had a connection with the PFF. There are plenty in this area.'

Kai made a sympathetic tutting sound. 'How old was the daughter?'

'Four or five,' said the woman. 'Not more.'

'Hey!' Leaning over the rope, Kai reached out and snapped his fingers at the closest militia guard. 'Any news of the daughter?'

The guard turned, scowling. He eyed Kai suspiciously before taking a step towards him. 'What daughter would that be then?'

Kai gestured towards the woman beside him. 'She says they had a daughter.'

'She?'

Kai twisted round. Where, just before, the woman had been standing, there were now a couple of elderly looking men pressing up against the cordon. The woman was nowhere to be seen. He shrugged. 'There was a woman there a few moments ago.'

'And why would the daughter be any concern of yours?' The militiaman moved closer. He squinted at Kai, then at Clod, then back to Kai again. 'You look familiar to me. Don't I know you from somewhere?'

'No, officer. I'd remember if we'd met.' Kai beamed his most innocent smile. 'Any clues about the killers?'

'*Killers?*' The militiaman glowered. 'What makes you think there's more than one?'

Kai nodded at the corpses. 'That's quite a lot of damage for one person with a knife.'

The militiaman came closer still. 'And how would you know the murder weapon was a knife?'

'I heard the sergeant . . .' said Kai.

The militiaman threw a sceptical glance in the direction of the officer. He was right over on the far side of the street. 'You heard the sergeant?'

'Well it wasn't a gun,' said Kai. 'That's obvious even from this distance. The woman has had her throat slashed.'

The militiaman lunged, grabbing Kai's wrist. 'Some of

101

the knife wounds, as it happens, were made by someone your height.' He beckoned to a colleague. 'Call the lieutenant over.'

'What's going on?' said Kai.

The militiaman reached for the handcuffs at his belt. 'You seem to know rather too much for your own good.'

'I'd love to help,' said Kai, 'but I've got my own investigating to do.' With brutal force he slammed his foot into the guard's shin.

The militiaman yelped, left go of Kai's wrist, and crumpled.

'No hard feelings,' said Kai. 'But you would only have been wasting your time. It wasn't me.' Dragging Clod behind him, he ducked away into the crowd.

There were some advantages to not yet being fully grown. Ease of slipping through crowds was one. When push came to shove, it was always possible to slide between people's legs. The militia were yelling as they barged their way through the crowd. But Kai and Clod had already reached the end of the street, where numbers were thinning. As Kai looked back to gauge how far ahead of the pursuers they were, he spotted a familiar face. The pretty eyes spotted him at the same time.

With a quick, nervous glance towards the approaching militiamen, Topaz beckoned to Kai.

19

Comrades

The room was basic and dimly lit. Bare plaster walls, tired revolutionary posters. Little furniture to speak of, a couple of plain low stools and some mats and cushions on the floor.

A haze of cigarette smoke filled the air. The oil lamp and candle that provided illumination, each had a halo. In one corner several small children were sleeping. Everyone else sat on the floor around a low table in the middle of the room. They spoke in hushed voices. There were cups and coffee pots on the table.

Standing in the doorway, Kai nodded a greeting and nudged Clod to do the same. Apart from the sleepers, everyone appeared to be older than him. Most were adults. Everyone was dressed in the combat fatigues of the Portobellan Freedom Fighters. No point expecting formal introductions.

From the small adjacent kitchen, Topaz handed both boys glasses of hot coffee.

Kai took a sip. *Mmmm*. It was thick, strong and sweet. Just what he needed. He thanked her.

'You're welcome.' She smiled warmly. 'So what's going on? How come you and your friend here were being pursued by the militia?'

'We were curious about the murders like everyone else,'

said Kai. 'I made the mistake of asking a question. Next thing I know, some dumb eager militiaman decided I was prime suspect material.'

'Morons!' Topaz scowled. 'What chance is there of them ever solving anything?'

There was little love lost between freedom fighters and the militia.

'Were the victims friends...' Kai corrected himself, '...*comrades* of yours?'

Topaz nodded. 'Shola in particular. She recruited me into the organization.' Tears brimmed in Topaz's sad brown eyes. 'She was like a big sister to me.'

'I'm sorry.' Kai touched her hand. 'The deaths looked grisly. Do your people have ideas about who did this?'

'Yes.' Topaz lowered her voice, confidentially. 'This was Nebula's work.'

'Nebula?' Kai saw Clod's eyes widen.

Topaz nodded. 'The assassin was a Neb. A youth, we think.'

'How come?'

Topaz pointed to a young girl lying curled up on a mat, her head on a woman's lap. The woman was stroking her. 'Izzy is Shola's daughter. She was sleeping in a small roof space above her parents' bedroom. She witnessed the whole thing.'

'Poor girl!' Kai shook his head. 'She's going to be having some nightmares.'

'She'll get plenty of love,' said Topaz. 'We're all one family in the PFF. She will be well looked after.'

'Did the as-s-sassin t-t-take anything?' It was the first time Clod had spoken.

Topaz stared at him in surprise. Her demeanour changed quickly. 'Why would an assassin do that?' Prickly.

'Trying, perhaps, to make it look like something else,' suggested Kai. He glared at Clod. *Stay silent*. 'A dispute, for example, between two factions of freedom fighters?'

Topaz frowned. 'As a matter of fact, some weapons were stolen.'

'Weapons?' said Kai. 'Tell me.'

'Why are you so interested?'

'Something might turn up in the bars or with one of the dealers.' Kai was thinking on his feet, and fast too. 'If this assassin was Nebulese like you say, they're hardly going to cart weapons all the way back to Nebula.'

'You think they might just dump them?'

'Bound to,' said Kai. 'If they're smart they'll do it somewhere no one will find them. But if they're in a hurry, they could just ditch them.'

Topaz considered the idea. She beckoned Kai towards the kitchen. 'As a matter of fact,' she whispered, lowering her voice, 'a new cache of automatics, assault rifles, grenades and explosives had just been delivered.'

Kai nodded. 'Something big going down?'

Topaz scowled. 'You know better than to ask. Two rifles, some grenades and an automatic went missing. All *kombatordnantz*, state-of-the-art stuff.'

'Wow!' Kai felt his skin prickle. Concealed beneath his hoodie, at the base of his spine, sat the *XK7*. He glanced at Clod. *Time to go*. 'If I see anything,' he assured Topaz, 'I'll let you know.'

20

Smell the Coffee

The sun was shining. Already crowded, the piazza bustled with stallholders and shoppers.

Spotting Clod on the steps of the Green Star Noodle Bar, Kai quickened his lazy pace.

Clod gestured to a pavement table. 'I brewed a p-p-pot of the strongest c-c-coffee. Thought you might n-n-need some!'

Ignoring the dig, Kai peered inside the bar.

'It's OK,' said Clod. 'Paps is d-d-down the warehouse all morning.' Tapping his nose, he gave Kai a wink. 'On b-b-business.'

Kai hesitated. 'You're sure?'

'Positive,' said Clod, pulling back a chair.

The two boys seated themselves.

Clod poured coffee. 'So how did you s-s-sleep?'

'I lay down on the sand and closed my eyes. How about you?'

'Very f-f-funny!'

'OK.' Kai smiled. 'Not bad. Not well. And certainly not enough.' He leant forwards, inhaling the aroma of coffee. 'Mmmm! Just what the doctor ordered. I got up early this morning and went for a swim. The sea was as still as a millpond. Not a ripple. Beautiful.'

Clod grinned. 'Perhaps the storm wave has been p-p-postponed?'

'I don't think so,' said Kai. 'Last night I heard the sound again. Twice. First when I was in the Old Neptune listening to stories. And then again on the beach when I was trying to sleep. Both times the groans were longer than before. And now they're coming closer together.'

Clod chewed his thumbnail.

Kai sipped his coffee. He had lain awake most of the night, his mind puzzling over the events of the previous twenty-four hours. Part of him was already on the hunt for the Nebulese fugitives. Already being drawn back into his old Downtown routines. But another part had been trying to weigh up the alternatives. This morning he had tried out the *XK7* underwater. And it worked. Didn't he have everything he needed now? He could just return to the headland and wait for the wave . . .

'So wh-wh-who are you today?' Clod poured more coffee. 'Bodysurfer or b-b-bounty hunter?'

'Both.' Kai smiled at how closely Clod had read his mind. 'As long as I'm waiting for the wave, I figure I may as well keep both options open.'

'Then the hunt is on?'

Kai nodded and cracked his knuckles. 'I was thinking about last night . . .' He glanced at the people sitting nearby. 'Maybe our fugitives overheard a couple of freedom fighters discussing their shiny new shipment of guns.'

Clod nodded. 'I've been th-th-thinking about that too. If it was th-th-them, did the g-g-girl wait outside, keeping watch?'

'Instinct tells me no,' said Kai. 'If she'd been with him on the job, she'd have at least been inside the flat guarding the door. And she wasn't. We know that. The little girl, Izzy, who watched it all, would have mentioned

107

her. There was no one to help him carry the guns and grenades.'

'Where w-w-was she then?'

Kai shrugged. 'They might have separated for safety. She might be injured. Already dead, even. She might be guarding their lair. Maybe they split tasks. He went to find weapons. She had to find food. They will need to eat and drink.' He waved towards the market. 'She's probably out there, right in front of our noses. Food shopping.'

Clod stiffened.

'What?' Kai turned to see a familiar face with eyeless sockets approaching through the crowd.

As Mushirah drew closer, Clod shifted uneasily in his seat.

'She's harmless,' whispered Kai, leaning close.

Clod said nothing.

'Greetings, masters!' Mushirah bowed.

'Good morning,' said Kai.

Mushirah held out her palm. 'I can tell you something.'

Clod twitched and hurriedly pressed a coin into Mushirah's palm. 'M-m-make it quick. We have important m-m-matters to discuss.'

Turning her eyeless sockets towards him, Mushirah chuckled. 'It does not concern you.'

Clod scowled.

Mushirah turned to Kai. 'I spoke falsely to you before.'

Clod snorted. 'An honest st-st-start!'

'Here's something for nothing.' Mushirah crouched beside Kai and leant in towards him, confidentially. 'Never trust a friend.'

'That's n-n-nice,' said Clod.

'You get what you pay for,' snapped Mushirah. 'I'll tell *you* something for nothing too, young master. Medusa whispers to me. The sea is coming. The ocean will rise up.'

Clod glanced at Kai. 'You're n-not the only one who thinks so.'

With quite sudden force, Mushirah gripped Kai's hand. The eyeless sockets seemed to glare. '*You are as good as dead in Downtown!*'

Kai held the eyeless gaze, stunned for a moment by the vehemence and the message. 'And what, pray, did you tell me that was false?'

Clod twitched uncomfortably.

Mushirah smiled. 'That you were unique.'

'I should have known!' Kai chuckled. His scepticism and wariness had been well placed. She had been playing with him from the start. 'So you were flattering me?'

'No!' Mushirah scowled. Indignant. 'But since we spoke, you and I, two strangers crossed my path. A boy and girl. The boy was afraid of me. Restless and eager to move on. He wouldn't come near. But the girl was curious.'

Mushirah's voice had softened. In an effort to catch what was being said, Clod shifted forwards.

Furtive and conspiratorial, Mushirah edged closer to Kai. 'She was exactly like you,' she whispered. 'Earth, water, air and fire – all four in equilibrium! And in her too, I detected something other.'

'One day you're special.' Kai shook his head. 'The next you're just like everyone else!'

Mushirah frowned and fell silent, seeming to drift away in contemplation of what all this might portend for the order of things. Suddenly her face brightened again. 'A real pretty thing!'

'The girl?' said Kai. 'How could you tell?'

Mushirah chuckled. 'Hoh! This interests him!' Grinning her toothless grin she held out her hands and wriggled her long, bony fingers. 'From the contours of her face! How else?'

Something nagged at the back of Kai's mind. 'Strangers, you said?'

'From Nebula.'

'*What!?*' A bolt of electricity shot through his body. 'How can you know that?'

'I have ears!' Mushirah chuckled. 'And I listen. No two people speak exactly alike. The accents were quite distinct.'

Kai and Clod exchanged glances. 'It's them,' hissed Kai. 'It has to be!' His mind was racing. 'Mushirah, this is so important. I have to find this boy and girl.'

Mushirah nodded. 'I think you do.'

'Is there anything you can tell me that would help? Something else about their appearance? Something I could identify?'

Mushirah shrugged then shook her head. 'Oh, there was one small thing . . .' Mushirah frowned. 'A flower pattern on the cuff of her sleeve.' She indicated the size with her thumb and forefinger. 'Embroidered.'

Kai sighed. 'It's not much to go on . . .'

'But it's a st-st-start,' said Clod.

'How long ago did you speak to them?' said Kai.

'Just now,' said Mushirah.

'What!' Kai was up on his feet. 'Where?'

'Not spitting distance from this very spot.' The smile twisted on Mushirah's lips. She cocked her head to one side and held out her palm. 'I happened to hear where they were heading . . .'

21

Soukh

It was *the* place in Portobello to buy food. Here there were specialist stalls for fish, meat, cheeses, vegetables, fruit, herbs and spices. Like the market in the piazza it was crowded and busy. But here in the enormous old building with its peeling paintwork and high vaulted ceilings, there was protection from the sun. It was considerably cooler.

From a distance, Phoebe watched as Phoenix took his change from the greengrocer, thanked him and turned to look for her. He was smiling smugly, pleased with himself. He had just bought an assortment of vegetables, using money he had found alongside the stolen guns. Spotting her, he walked over and surreptitiously slipped her the package. 'Since you're not prepared to carry a weapon,' he said, speaking out of the corner of his mouth, 'you can carry the shopping!'

Phoebe glanced around. They had agreed to keep apart as much as possible when they were out in public, to make it harder for anyone who might be on the lookout for them. Right now, nobody appeared to be paying them undue attention. All well and good. 'How are we going to cook this stuff?'

'I thought we could fry the giltheads we caught, with garlic, spring onions, and ginger.' Phoenix nudged her playfully. 'What d'you reckon?'

Phoebe stamped on his foot.

He winced and grinned. 'Actually, fish is supposed to be better for you raw!'

Phoebe scowled. He was trying to reassure her. This was the old Phoenix, the caring, playful Phoenix. She wanted this one back.

'Don't worry,' he chuckled. 'We'll find a way.' He strode off.

Phoebe watched him move through the soukh. Nothing was turning out quite like it had been supposed to. She had thought she had known him so well. She had, hadn't she? But since they crossed the border, perhaps because of the pressures of being on the run, he seemed to have changed. Had there been a darker side to him all along, which she just hadn't noticed?

Phoenix was almost strutting. So confident and self-assured with the gun hidden in the waistband of his trousers. Phoebe walked twenty paces behind. She felt like a sulking tot, dragging her feet. It made her nervous having guns around. The truth was, it made her nervous now having *him* around.

When he'd returned with the weapons, he had boasted he'd stolen them without disturbing a soul. And she hadn't believed him. When she'd probed about the exact circumstances – where he had gone, how he'd known where to find guns, what had actually happened – he had become evasive like a small child. She could tell he was lying. Why?

Phoenix paused in front of a fish stall, waiting for Phoebe to catch up. 'Cheer up,' he whispered. 'You're scowling too much. You'll scare people!'

Phoebe scowled more.

Phoenix touched her hand. 'Come on. It's not so bad.'

112

She moved away and turned her back on him. It was stupid taking risks like that in public. She pretended to be interested in some lobsters.

'We'll lie low for a few days more,' said Phoenix. 'Eat well. Get our strength up. At night we'll go out and scout around. Check out the headland. Find ourselves an escape route.'

'The old woman said there was no way out of here.'

'What would she know?' Phoenix laughed. 'She was blind!'

Glancing back to where Clod was standing, Kai shook his head. Yet another disappointment. The girl buying shellfish was plumper than Mushirah's description. The boy had looked too tall. And beneath her veil the girl's nose had been quite pronounced – surely Mushirah would have remarked on this? Kai had wondered if it might have been some sort of disguise, but the girl had no flowers on her cuffs. It wasn't her.

Clod was signalling. Kai turned to check what he was indicating. Dragging her feet, a forlorn-looking figure, hair covered by a veil, shuffled between the fish stalls. She had her back to him and was heading away. He would have to overtake to get a look.

The girl had stopped at another stall. She was examining lobsters. As Kai approached, a boy, slim build like her, strong and athletic looking, bumped into her, smiled, said a few words then continued on his way. Kai was near and closing. He felt the hairs prickle on the back of his neck. There was decoration on the girl's cuff. Flowers!

Spinning around, Kai caught Clod's eye and signalled for him to watch the boy. Then, moving up close, he took another good look at the girl's cuffs. He stretched forwards

113

to examine the crustaceans and glanced back at her face.

For the briefest of moments her eyes made contact with his. Framed in the shadows of her veil, the haunting face he'd glimpsed underwater stared back at him. It was her! She was the fugitive girl. He was instantly, doubly sure of it. And in that electrifying split second, he was sure of something else – *she recognized him too*. Averting her face, she pretended to be interested in some fish on the far side of the stall. She moved over to examine them more closely. The fishmonger followed her.

Kai watched and listened. If the girl had an accent it was so slight as to be unnoticeable. Had Mushirah been right? Was this girl Nebulese? Perhaps she was just a girl from the other side of town. Portobello was a big city, there were plenty of faces he had never seen. Studying her outline for bulges that might conceal a weapon, he saw her glance at him again. This time her face was blank. She was holding a package that looked like some vegetables in a bag. Her face was bewitching. But was it the right girl?

Phoebe did her best to walk briskly, without it looking like she was in a hurry. *Where was Phoenix?* The last she'd seen of him, he'd been heading towards the exit. She had been unable to keep an eye on him because of the boy watching her so closely.

Without halting, Phoebe looked back over her shoulder. The boy was there, still standing at the fish stall on the corner. Staring after her. She quickened her pace to match her accelerating heartbeat.

Phoenix was suddenly there, leaning against the wall by the exit. Nonchalant. Smiling. Waiting patiently. Phoebe could feel the eyes of the boy boring into her back, watching her every move. She thought of changing direction, but Phoenix would only come hurrying after her. Instead she scowled and tried discreetly to wave him away. But Phoenix was walking towards her, confused by her signals.

'What's going on?'

'Don't come any closer!' Phoebe glared.

Phoenix frowned and glanced around.

'Look past me, over my shoulder,' snapped Phoebe. She paused at the stall by the exit, pretending to take an interest in their bundles of fresh herbs. 'See a boy by the fish stall, staring this way?'

'Uh-huh.' Phoenix nodded.

'Recognize him?'

'No.'

'Well, I do,' said Phoebe. 'He's the one I saw underwater.'

Phoenix stiffened. 'You're kidding me?'

'No,' hissed Phoebe. 'Deadly serious. He was watching me. He came right up close.'

'You think he's on to us?'

'I don't know.' There was panic in her voice. She could feel it rising.

Phoenix swore under his breath. 'One way or another, we could be about to find out.' His hand moved to his waistband. 'He's coming this way!'

Blood pounded in Phoebe's ears. As she started to turn, a hint of a smirk crept across Phoenix's lips. She twisted round to see what was amusing him.

A small boy, no more than a toddler, was staggering towards them on unsteady feet. His mother, still at the fish stall on the corner, called out to him to wait.

Phoebe scanned the market hall in vain. The boy from the beach had vanished.

22

As Good As Dead

Kai pushed Clod into the alcove.

'Is it h-h-her?' said Clod.

Kai nodded. 'I'm certain. Did you watch the boy?'

Clod nodded. 'It l-l-looked to me like he has s-something under his j-j-jacket.'

'An automatic?'

'I th-th-think so.'

'The girl doesn't, as far as I can tell.' Kai peered out from behind the alcove's ornamental pillar. The boy and girl were standing very near one another, close to the entrance. 'Quick!' Kai tugged Clod's jacket. 'Take this off!'

'*What?*'

'She's seen me. I need to swap with you. She recognized me. Come on.'

Grudgingly, Clod obeyed. Kai tried to hurry him.

Checking to make sure no one was watching, Kai whipped off his own jacket and the top he was wearing beneath. He tossed Clod the clothes he had removed and hurriedly pulled on the dark brown hoodie he snatched off Clod. He glanced again from behind the pillar. 'They're leaving!'

'What w-w-will you do?'

'Go after them, of course.' With Clod's top on, Kai struggled to move. It was too tight around the shoulders,

116

too baggy lower down. And, putting on Kai's top, Clod was having problems in reverse. But there wasn't time to change back now. Kai tugged on the hood. It just about stretched to cover his eyes. As long as he didn't move his shoulders. It would have to do. 'Dressed like this,' he groaned, 'I should at least gain the element of surprise!'

Phoebe almost had to run to keep up with Phoenix. They had been moving swiftly through the streets of Downtown. Weaving their way through the labyrinth. Now they were in yet another narrow street of compact shabby-looking houses. She had lost all sense of direction. 'Where are we heading?'

'I'm not sure exactly.' Phoenix glanced back over his shoulder. 'But if it really was the boy you thought you saw before, and he's back there somewhere, watching and following us, we can't afford to lead him to our hiding place.'

'OK,' she panted. 'Let's pause for a minute. See if he is. There's no point hurrying if he's not. We're only drawing attention to ourselves.'

Phoenix looked around and shrugged. 'OK.' Discreetly he reached under his jacket. With a double click he released the safety catch and cocked the gun ready to fire. There was an adrenalinized glint in his eye. 'What does this boy look like?'

Phoebe peered back up the street they had just run down. 'Your sort of height, maybe not quite as tall. Unruly hair. Wearing a short jalabi hooded top.'

'What colour?'

'A faded blue.'

'Can't see anyone fitting that description.' Phoenix pulled his hood down further to shade his eyes. 'But there's

117

a youth in a scruffy dark brown number coming up the street. You're sure it was faded blue?'

'Where?' Phoebe followed his gaze. At the far end of the street, hidden amongst the other pedestrians going about their business, a boy was slowly ambling his way towards them, hugging the walls, keeping to the shadows. She couldn't see his face, and the top wasn't the one he'd been wearing earlier but . . . She grabbed Phoenix's arm. 'Oh God! I think it's him.'

'You *think*?'

'No.' She had watched the boy sauntering round the fish stall. The lazy, easy style he had of walking, it was the same. 'I'm sure. What are we going to do?'

'Wait for him.' Phoenix nodded calmly towards the top of the street. There was a water fountain set at one corner. 'Let's take a drink. He can come to us.'

'We don't know what he wants,' said Phoebe. Her voice trembled. 'We know nothing about him. He might not even be looking for us.' But she knew, as she said it, this could not be true. It was the same boy she had seen in the water. And at the fish stall, when he'd stared at her, she had seen the recognition in his eyes. He was following them.

'Come off it, sis! He's *hunting* us.'

Phoebe had no comeback. *Why didn't she feel hunted?* Something she'd seen in his face had seemed so . . . gentle. And now as she looked into Phoenix's eyes, excited violence was all she saw.

The sun was high in the sky. Kai felt sweat creeping beneath his hair. It formed rivulets and began to trickle down his scalp. And there were droplets making their way through his eyebrows; he could see them preparing to drip

118

into his eyes. He had to resist the urge to wipe them – not that he could easily raise his arms in Clod's tight woollen top. It was important not to make any sudden movements that might look aggressive. *Or like he was reaching for a gun.*

The two Neb fugitives were sitting with their backs to him, on the edge of a small drinking fountain, scooping up water and slaking their thirst. The boy was no longer hooded, and the girl's veil rested on her shoulders. They had pale skin. The girl had short fair hair, like the boy. They might easily be brother and sister. Kai only had to whip out the *XK7* and – pop pop – they would be lying there dead. Job done. He could collect his reward.

Then a whole new life would open up for him. A life away from Downtown. The life he had always dreamt of. A life without ever-present violence and danger. A life with some of the freedoms that others, elsewhere in the world, took for granted.

But this wasn't like other contracts. He felt uneasy. There were too many unknowns. He felt too much curiosity. He was *intrigued*. He knew he wouldn't kill them unless he had to. And that was bad.

Small children were playing, running in and out of doorways, chasing one another, kicking a ball back and forth across the street. Old men sat on stools in the shade. Mothers and grandmothers chattered from doorsteps and balconies.

As Kai approached the two fugitives, the world seemed to slow. Or his mind speeded up. He was sensing everything with a vividness and crystal clarity. There was a bitter taste in his mouth. His heart was speeding up. How might they react? Where, if it came to it, might they run? He was considering every eventuality . . .

The girl glanced up. Looking into his face, she smiled and said something to the boy beside her. The boy twisted round. There was a gun in his hand. A look of horror swept the smile from the girl's face. Flames leapt from the barrel of the gun.

BAM-BAM-BAM . . .

Reflexes took over. As the gun flashed and the air filled with deafening noise, Kai dived.

BAM-BAM-BAM . . .

Sailing through the air, bullets balletically passed him by.

BAM-BAM-BAM . . .

All except one.

BAM!

Pain exploded in Kai's arm with the force of a rocket. Catching him mid-flight, it flipped him head over heels, once, twice, three times. A splayed, spinning rag doll, he cartwheeled across the cobbles. And crumpled.

Bright sunshine seeped away. The world faded and inky darkness rushed in to take its place. This was it.

Silence. Emptiness.

As good as dead in Downtown.

The street appeared empty. Old men, children, mothers and grandmothers – all had vanished. They had either ducked indoors or thrown themselves on the ground.

The boy from the beach lay motionless on the ground.

Phoenix had stopped firing and was trying to reload the automatic. He was struggling with a jammed magazine.

Phoebe's ears still rang from the deafening gunfire. She had screamed non-stop throughout, but never heard her own voice. She grabbed Phoenix's arm. 'What are you *doing*?'

'What does it look like?' Phoenix glared and shoved her away.

120

'You *idiot*!' Phoebe snatched the gun from his hands. 'You asked me to tell you if he was holding a gun!'

Phoenix grabbed her wrist. 'And you said no!'

'So you shot him?'

Laughing, Phoenix prised the gun from Phoebe's hand. 'In this world, it's who shoots first.' This time he rammed the magazine successfully into position and loaded a round into the breach. 'Now let's go see how we did.'

The boy from the beach hadn't moved. The shoulder of his top was dark with blood.

Pointing the gun at his head, Phoenix edged the toe of his boot underneath the chest and rolled the body over.

Blinking open his eyes, Kai saw two blurry shapes. Pain was shouting for attention all over his body, screaming from his shoulder. He was lying on his back, on something hard. He recognized the voice of the girl from the soukh. She was one of the fuzzy figures above him. He forced his eyes into focus. She was yelling at the boy with the gun.

'Hey!' The boy was sneering. 'Whaddya know? The wretch is still alive!' He pointed the gun at Kai's head.

Kai saw the finger tightening on the trigger.

'*No!*' The girl's foot sliced upwards, crunching into hand and gun.

BAM!

Kai rolled. Painfully. Over and over, till he hit a wall. Scrambling to his feet, he saw the girl was lying on the ground. So was the gun. The boy was reaching for it. Half hobbling, Kai ran till he reached a doorway and threw himself inside.

BAM!

Plaster and timber splintered.

BAM-BAM-BAM!

121

Choking dust filled the porch. Kai groped for the *XK7*. His right arm was numb and useless, covered in blood, but his left hand found the cold metal.

BAM-BAM-BAM!

Fragments of plaster and timber rained down on him. Outside in the street, the boy was yelling at the girl as he fired. Kai aimed and pulled the trigger.

BOOM!

The recoil from the gun knocked him off balance. The shot missed its target, but the boy and girl hit the dirt.

BOOM!

BAM-BAM!

BOOM-BOOM-BOOM!

23

Angels with Guns

BOOM ... BOOM ... BOOM ...

Kai jerked into consciousness, shaking with panic. What was going on? Where was he? What was that sound?

Oh! Stupid! He breathed a sigh of relief. It was only the gentle, steady, trembling beat of his own heart.

He had been hit. He recalled the deafening roar of handguns, automatics ... bullets exploding all around him, everywhere and then ...

Suddenly, he realized what it was that had startled him. Another sound – not his own heartbeat, not even the remembered cacophony of the gun battle, but the now familiar harsh grunts and groans from deep beneath the ocean. Louder and stronger than he had ever heard them. The sound had shaken him, scared him.

And where was he?

Lying on his back in a dark place.

What had happened?

He tried to recall ...

Back to the gunfire. The wound in his shoulder. Sheltering in a porch. He and the boy shooting at each other. The rounds in the *XK7* had been so powerful he had found it hard to control the gun with his uninjured left hand. Gradually the boy and girl had crawled behind the fountain and edged their way towards the end of the street. Every time he had tried to take a shot, the boy had forced him back behind cover with a barrage of bullets. So he had just sat back, clutched his bloody wound, and waited.

A chilling silence had filled the street. Slowly the air had cleared of smoke, dust and noise. Tentatively, he had peered out, only to glimpse the two fugitives at the far end of the street, vanishing round the corner. His shoulder had screamed with every movement, but he had scrambled to his feet and staggered after them. Somewhere nearby sirens had been wailing, the militia – alerted and closing in. Heads of hiding citizens lifted as he loped up the street.

He was reliving it.

XK7 in hand, stumbling down the alley in pursuit. More bullets whistling towards him as he rounded the corner. Instinctively, he threw himself to the ground, excruciating pain searing down his right side. The boy was yelling at the girl. Lifting his face from the dirt, he saw the boy grab her wrist and start to run, dragging her after him. He raised the *XK7* to take a shot, but something stopped him.

What . . .?

The boy was keeping the girl close behind him *as a shield*. Still firing above the heads of pedestrians, to keep them out of his way, he had continued to loose off rounds at Kai too. Slowly but surely the boy and girl were heading back towards the southern end of the harbour and the sea.

Without realizing it, he had been getting weaker. But dizzy and out of breath, he had forced himself to try and catch up. So he had not been very far behind when the two of them had run out of a side street into the harbourside area.

What had happened next was burned into his memory.

A warning had been shouted. 'Militia! Freeze! You're under arrest!' Then the air had roared and crackled with a hail of gunfire the like of which he had never witnessed before. The militia must have anticipated where the running gun battle was heading, got there ahead of them and taken up positions. But the boy and girl were fortunate – the militia never had and never would win prizes for their marksmanship.

The fugitives had ducked back into the alley, apparently unscathed. Glancing round, the girl had seen Kai staggering towards them. He had halted and raised the *XK7* to aim, but he'd been shaking so badly he'd had to lower his arm. The boy meanwhile had snapped a fresh magazine into his automatic, grabbed hold of the girl's hand and dragged her, charging out on to the harbourside a second time.

Suicide!

In fluid synchronized movements, they had zigzagged, dived and rolled, the boy shooting as he ran. Weaving a path through the bullets, they had crossed the ground with such astonishing speed and agility that many of the militia ceased shooting and gawped in stunned amazement.

Dodging everything the militia could fire at them, the fugitives had crossed the entire dockside before hurling themselves out over the harbour, into the water. Hurrying to the water's edge, twenty or more militiamen had stood blasting the sea with everything they had.

Kai had ducked between some crates. From here he had watched the militia as they waited for the boy and girl to surface. He had counted the seconds. The minutes. After just three, some of the militia had given them up for dead and started to walk away. Others had stayed watching the water a little longer. Five, six, seven minutes even. He had kept counting till his own breath-holding limit was reached. Then he must have passed out.

Or was he dead?

The thought hit him like a rock falling from the sky.

He was looking down on himself – wasn't this what was supposed to happen at death? He was above his own body. It lay on top of some sacks, pale, limp and lifeless. Several figures knelt around him, bright light emanating from their brows. Were they angels? Kai looked more closely. They were armed with handguns and compact assault rifles. *Angels with guns?*

While one propped his head on something soft, another cut away the clothing from around the disgusting wound. The bent-over figure began to clean and examine the hole: dark coagulated blood and ruptured flesh. A syringe appeared and was plunged into his arm.

Kai felt himself shudder and shake. Suddenly he was back in his own body. A bright light was shining in his face. Behind the light a figure in silhouette.

'Do you know who I am?' The voice was strong and gentle.

Kai squinted against the light. 'God does not exist.'

'Oh?'

'So you must be . . . Mendel.'

'Excellent.' The light was redirected. Mendel's face became visible. He and his agents were all wearing headbands with small, bright built-in lights. 'You're back in the land of the living.' He chuckled. 'Conscious and wisecracking.'

'Where are we?'

'Downtown,' said Mendel. 'In a warehouse just off the main concourse.'

Kai tried to sit up. '*Argh!*' He couldn't move. Pain stabbed his right shoulder. Something or somebody was holding him down.

'Keep still,' said Mendel. 'The medics are trying their best to repair you.'

'I'm injured?' Of course. He had forgotten.

126

'You were lucky. This type of high-velocity round tends to make mincemeat of the human body. You've scarcely more than a graze – minor damage to skin and muscle tissue. You're young and fit. You might even get away without a scar.'

'It was the boy.' Kai winced. 'How come you're here? How did you find me?'

'I was concerned.' Mendel held up the *XK7* which Kai had taken from him. 'Built-in transmitter. The tracker reported it hadn't moved all afternoon. Didn't think you'd have left the gun on the dockside while you took a nap. When we got here after dark, we found you inside a pile of crates.' He pointed. 'Just up the street.'

The sound of a loud explosion startled Kai. It was some way off, but still big enough to shake the building.

'The PFF on a spree,' explained Mendel. 'That's the fourth bomb today.' He sighed wearily and shook his head. 'Couldn't have come at a worse time.'

'It's retaliation,' said Kai. 'Fugitive boy killed some freedom fighters. He only wanted their weapons but now the PFF think Nebula is sending highly trained young assassins against them.'

'Not such a bad idea,' said Mendel. 'After today's attacks those terrorist cells are doomed. We know their locations, thanks to a new informant. The president will inevitably order massive retaliation. Unfortunately that might make it harder for us to keep in contact with you.'

Kai snorted. 'What makes you think I'm prepared to work for you?'

Mendel smiled at the obstinacy. 'Clearly you have already been doing so. We have to leave you now. But you've been well patched up. Let me remind you – on this job the clock is ticking fast.'

24

Curfew

'*Get off the streets!*' The militia patrol car, with flashing lights and loudspeakers on its roof, cruised at a crawl around the piazza. '*Get off the streets NOW. There are a few minutes remaining till curfew enforcement. Get off the streets. The militia have strict orders to ARREST ANYONE found outdoors after ten o'clock tonight.*'

Keeping one eye on a militia foot patrol hanging around the far corner, Kai crossed the piazza, making his way towards the Green Star Noodle Bar. A few dark shadows flickered around the piazza's edges as Downtowners scurried home. Familiar mouthwatering smells – frying onions, spices, fish and noodles – wafted across the empty square, but the Green Star's streetside tables were empty and the usual lively hubbub was absent.

Watching from the top of the steps, Clod nodded as he recognized Kai. 'You're still alive then!' He beckoned. 'You'd b-better come in.'

'What about Paps?'

'Away on b-b-business again.' Clod winked. 'New client. Not back yet, so l-l-looks like he won't be home till d-d-dawn.'

Kai surveyed the empty square.

'*Anyone on the streets after ten will be arrested,*' blared the patrol-car speakers. '*Get off the streets NOW!*'

128

'Doesn't look like you've g-g-got a lot of choice,' said Clod. 'Come on. I'll f-f-fix you some food.'

The stench of rotting fish was so all-pervading, Phoebe had long since grown used to it. But whenever, like now, she slipped out on deck for a while to take a breather and inhale some fresher air, she found herself trying to delay as long as possible the moment when she had to return to the dingy fetid space below deck. She and Phoenix had escaped one kind of confinement only to be trapped in another; self imposed, but far more unsavoury. She wondered how long she would be able to endure it.

The militia's announcements had ceased. For a few brief moments the night had been beautifully, unbelievably still. Then an electronically amplified siren had croaked into life. It rose now in pitch and volume, filling the night air. Its wail barrelled through the empty streets of Downtown, echoing out across the harbour. Phoebe gave a start as the boat shuddered. A dripping silhouette emerged from the water at the stern.

Whites of eyes and teeth glistened in the moonlight. 'It's curfew time,' Phoenix grinned, breathless. 'I've checked – the streets are deserted. Time for a little night trip.'

'What about the militia?' said Phoebe.

'Dolts with obsolete weapons!' Phoenix laughed. 'We're not going to let them ruin our fun.'

Kai and Clod sat at a table on the balcony, picking over the remains of a meal. The curfew siren had done its wailing. People had hurried home and the streets had emptied. But there was still no sign of Paps.

Kai had filled Clod in on his pursuit of the fugitives, the bullet that had wounded his shoulder and ruined Clod's brown hooded top, and his second encounter with the SIA. As a militia patrol sauntered past, machine guns jutting from hips, Kai plucked a fishbone from between his teeth. 'This crackdown isn't going to make a scrap of difference.'

'The Nebs always retaliate,' said Clod.

Kai nodded. 'And this time they know the location of the PFF's cells. They're going to wipe them out. They told me.'

Clod looked stunned.

Kai stared out into the darkness. Topaz was one of those freedom fighters.

'What is it?' said Clod.

'I was thinking – maybe I should warn them?'

'The PFF?'

Kai nodded.

Clod smirked. 'And one in p-p-particular, by any chance?'

'What d'you mean?'

Clod shrugged. 'Didn't I detect a little fr-fr-frisson between you and a certain fr-fr-freedom fighter?'

'Who? If you're talking about Topaz, I've known her since we were tiddlers. She's like a sister to me.'

'That's not what *her* eyes say!'

Kai scowled and folded his arms. 'Would you warn them, in my shoes?'

'Caring for her like a s-s-sister . . .' said Clod. 'Hmmm, let me think.' He rested his chin on his hands. His brow furrowed. 'No,' he said, sudden and decisive, 'unless you want to be l-l-lynched as a collaborator. How would you explain the fact that you've b-b-been talking to the Nebs? Did you think of that?'

Kai tutted. Clod was right.

'She and her comrades have ch-ch-chosen their path.

130

Death is something freedom fighters accept. In fact they w-w-welcome it apparently.' Clod gestured towards the narrow streets across the piazza. 'You've seen the murals glorifying their fallen. They're heroes and m-m-martyrs!'

Kai chewed a fingernail. 'Topaz is a good person.'

'Too young to d-d-die?'

Kai nodded. There had to be something he could do or say that would make a difference.

The two boys sat in silent frustration.

'M-m-maybe there's another way,' said Clod.

'Another way?' Kai studied Clod's face. 'There's a cunning twinkle in your eye. What are you thinking?'

'Mushirah,' said Clod.

Kai frowned, puzzled. 'I'm not with you.'

'She delivers pr-pr-prophecies.'

'So-called! And?'

'You could ask her to pr-pr-prophesy something that will keep T-T-Topaz away from harm.'

Kai's brow knotted. 'Deliver a prophecy to order? What makes you think Mushirah would do that?'

Clod half-squirmed, half-shrugged and looked away. 'I dunno, just a guess, I g-g-guess.'

'Clod, is there something you're not telling me?'

Clod shrugged, he was staring at his feet.

Kai's suspicions were raised. 'Has Mushirah done something like that for you?'

Clod bowed his head.

'Clod?'

After a long pause, Clod nodded. 'N-n-not me, exactly.'

'What did you ask her to prophesy?'

'Oh, just . . .' Clod's face had turned pale. 'N-n-nothing very much.'

'Tell me!'

Clod flinched and cringed. 'Please d-d-don't be angry.'

Kai leant close. '*Tell!*'

'It was P-P-Paps . . .' Clod's voice quivered. 'I had to.'

'Had to what?' snapped Kai. 'Spit it out!'

'I p-p-paid her,' said Clod, 'to p-p-persuade you to delay your l-l-leaving.'

Kai snarled. ' "You dream of escape," she said to me. "But you are not ready . . . there is something that you need . . . things you must do before leaving." '

Clod's eyes were wide with fear. He nodded.

Slumping back into his seat, Kai sat brooding in silence. He cracked his knuckles one by one. At the back of his mind, hadn't he always suspected as much? That Mushirah's prophecies were just empty ramblings? And that nobody should be trusted, least of all someone who called themselves friend. He'd been duped. What a fool. He grunted. 'Can you take me to her?'

Clod's nervous gaze darted out into the darkness. 'What! Now?'

Kai nodded. 'If it's to be of any use.'

'I s-s-suppose.'

'Good!' Jumping up, Kai tugged Clod to his feet. 'You *owe* me. Big time.' His hand gripped Clod's like a vice. 'Do this for me and maybe I'll forgive your betrayal.' Kai's grip tightened till Clod yelped. 'There won't be a second chance.'

25

Velvety Thickness

The night air was damp and smelt strongly of sea. With the curfew now in force, Downtown's streets were silent, empty and very, very dark. In this part of the city there was little street lighting. And tonight people had closed their shutters early and gone to bed. Darkness had settled on the town like a fog. It was warm and there was a rich velvety thickness to it, as if you might wrap it round yourself or snuggle up against it.

Striding through the deserted streets, Phoebe should have felt safer than she had for days – Phoenix, armed and deadly at her side, the pair of them with the city to themselves. But she was scared of him. More scared of him now than of the people shuttered away in their homes. More scared of him even than of the patrolling militia guards. And did she fear him more than the hunter boy – whose life she had tried to save, who had come after them with a gun . . . and, if he was still alive, would be doing so again?

Halting suddenly in mid-step, Phoenix held up a hand for silence.

Phoebe froze and held her breath. Coming towards them from the right, the unmistakable whine and grumble of diesel engines. Jeeps. They sounded like they were in a hurry. Had she and Phoenix been spotted and reported? Perhaps they'd taken the dark too much for granted.

'They're headed this way.' Phoenix's eyes flashed yellow in the darkness as he turned. 'Quick!'

Phoebe felt her shoulder almost yanked from its socket as Phoenix grabbed her wrist and took off running. With big bounding strides he loped through the night like some giant hare.

Portobello, Kai reflected, was as quiet as a sleeping village. He and Clod had crossed Downtown in the darkness without meeting a soul. Unless dogs had souls – which he doubted. One of Downtown's strays, unnerved by the eerie silence, had come whining for company, but he had shooed it away. And twice on their journey they had heard the sound of a militia patrol in a nearby street, but not once had they actually seen them.

They had climbed to the citadel, the northern quarter of Portobello, with its sturdy old buildings – government offices, municipal headquarters and the like. Towering over them and everything else stood the gleaming offices of the Nebulese corporations. Here they were only a couple of streets away from no-man's-land and the border fence.

Stopping in his tracks, Kai tugged Clod's sleeve and pointed towards a doorway. 'Could that be her?'

Clod peered. 'I can't see from here.'

As the two boys approached, what appeared to be a bundle of rags and old newspapers moved in a doorway. The dark shape of a head bobbed. The bundle grunted. 'What d'you want?' snapped a familiar voice. 'Can't an old woman be left in peace for one night?'

'*Shhhh!*' hissed Clod. 'Mushirah, we're n-n-not the authorities. We're not here to m-m-move you on.'

Mushirah made a humphing noise.

'We've come at great risk to ourselves,' said Kai. 'There's a curfew in force.'

'D'you think I don't know that?' said Mushirah, irritably. 'Well? What do you want?'

'A prophecy,' said Kai.

'It is coming,' said Mushirah. 'Did you not hear me before? The day is close at hand when the great wave will return.' Suddenly, she stretched up. 'Only stronger, higher and *meaner*.' Her gestures and expression emphasized her words. 'It will come, crushing everything in its path. And poor miserable, downtrodden Downtown shall be washed from the face of the earth. There!'

'Shhhh!' said Clod. 'D'you want the militia to f-f-find us?'

Kai put his hand on Mushirah's arm. 'What you say about the storm wave I know to be true. But not everything you prophesy is so.'

'What do you mean?'

'My friend here paid you for a falsehood,' said Kai.

'Not a falsehood,' said Mushirah. 'Because I am old and blind, do not mistake me for a fool. I know who you are. Of course I do! I've known you all your life. I recognized the footsteps of you and your friend before either of you opened your mouths to speak. All that I told you the other day was true. Because your friend paid me to say it and you paid me to hear it doesn't make it any less so. Everything Mushirah says comes to pass.'

Kai's body gave an involuntary shudder. It was *all* true? He rubbed his aching shoulder. 'I need you to make a prophecy to someone for me. I will pay you.'

'Tell me.'

'I want you to warn a freedom fighter about danger from Nebulese attack.'

'You have secret information?' Mushirah placed her hand on Kai's forehead.

'Yes,' said Kai.

'And it is true,' said Mushirah. 'Tell me their name and where to find them and you may consider it done.' She held out her hand for payment. 'But be warned – the freedom fighters have fire in their blood. They will not heed the words of a crazy old woman.'

'I know,' said Kai. 'But it's all I can do.'

Phoenix had a finger to his lips.

Still panting from the last sprint, Phoebe gulped air and held her breath. Over the booming of her pulse, she strained to listen. The jeeps had moved on. Now another sound disturbed the night.

Phoenix hissed a curse under his breath. 'Foot patrol.'

'*Two*,' said Phoebe. 'And by the sound of things coming in opposite directions!'

Phoenix jerked around. 'We have to hide! Quick!'

Phoebe scanned the square. To the left of them there was no cover, just open space and cobbles. To the right, a terrace of narrow town houses looking out on the piazza. A row of doors – all shut. Moving swiftly and silently, she tried a handle. *Locked*. And another. Phoenix tried too, in vain.

Phoebe felt panic rising. She looked around. *Where could they go?*

Phoenix was unclipping the assault rifle from his back. 'We're in trouble,' he said, snapping a magazine into the gun. He rested it against his shoulder. Ready.

'Not yet.' Phoebe pointed upwards. A short distance above her, no more than a couple of metres, a small balcony jutted out from the front of a first-floor apartment.

136

Beams of light – the powerful flashlights of one of the foot patrols – swept across the buildings further up the street. It would only be a matter of seconds before they rounded the corner. Down the other end of the street, lights were beginning to appear too.

Below the balcony, Phoebe cupped her hands and bent her legs. 'Come on!' she hissed.

Phoenix put down the handgun and assault rifle. Putting his foot in Phoebe's cupped palms, he placed his hands on her shoulder. 'Ready?'

Phoebe nodded.

'One, two, three . . .' As Phoebe heaved, Phoenix sprang.

Up the street, voices and footsteps were growing louder. Torch beams drifting closer. Hurriedly, Phoebe passed the guns up to her brother.

Hooking his feet round the railings, Phoenix dropped back, hanging upside down from the balcony. '*Climb!*' he hissed.

As Phoebe grabbed his wrists, a torch beam swept towards her. Twisting, she jerked her legs up, high as she could. Phoenix gasped. Clambering up his body, she clutched the cold metal railings and scrambled to safety. Moments later Phoenix was beside her, flat against the balcony floor.

On the ground below, the two patrols drew close and hailed one another.

In the darkness, Phoebe watched Phoenix's knuckles tighten on the gun.

Kai ran, looking back over his shoulder. The beam of the jeep's headlights was lighting up buildings on the corner behind. In a matter of seconds, he and Clod would be caught in its glare. '*Come on!*' he hissed. It was only a short run to the end of the street and the big wide piazza, but there was no way Clod would make it. He glanced around. Where could they hide?

Kai's eyes fell on a market stall cart he had just passed, parked up against one of the houses. Running over, he lifted the tarpaulin and beckoned. 'Hurry! In here!'

Clod staggered over, gasping for air. Without warning, Kai grabbed him from behind and hefted him up over the side of the cart. In the next moment he was over the side himself and tumbling down on top. As the jeep's headlights blazed down the street, he yanked the tarpaulin over.

Three jeeps crawled by. Their engines, fortunately, were loud enough to mask Clod's gasps for air. Peering through a crack in the side of the cart, Kai watched the patrol reach the top of the street, turn into the square, then abruptly halt. He swore under his breath.

'What?' croaked Clod.

'They're stopping. They're getting out.'

'Are they coming this way?'

'No,' said Kai. 'But there are other militiamen there, chatting to them. Looks like they've met up with a foot patrol.'

Phoenix crouched at the bars of the balcony, muttering under his breath.

Phoebe tried to convince herself she was shaking from cold, not fear. 'We should just wait for them to leave,' she whispered.

Phoenix shook his head. 'They're drinking. We could be here for the night. The longer we wait, the greater the danger.'

Phoebe said nothing. What was the point? Phoenix was convinced that with the militia making so much noise, it was only a matter of time before people in one of the apartments looked out and spotted them there, on the balcony. Perhaps he was right. She felt sure they stood a better chance staying where they were, but it made no difference – he had long since ceased listening to her.

Phoenix was already over the rail and perched on the edge. Down on the ground the militiamen had positioned the three jeeps so that their headlights illuminated a small patch of ground. Here the men sat or stood, laughing and chatting, passing round a bottle, rolling cigarettes and smoking.

Phoenix pointed. 'They've posted a couple of guards to keep watch,' he whispered. 'But they're only half-hearted. They keep returning to the group for a drag on a cigarette and a slug of drink.'

Phoebe saw the silhouetted guard nearest them making his way back towards the group in the light.

'You're sure you won't take a gun?'

Phoebe nodded.

'OK,' said Phoenix. 'Wait for me to get into position. Then, if the guard is still distracted, come straight after.'

As Phoebe nodded, Phoenix touched her hand. His touch made her shiver. She tried to disguise it, but Phoenix had seen it. She caught the look in his eye as he jumped.

'*Aagh!*' Clod twisted and grabbed at his foot.

'*Shhh!*' Kai turned. 'What's up?' In the almost total darkness Kai could scarcely make out Clod's features, but he knew he wasn't smiling.

'Cr-cr-cramp!'

'Which foot?'

'Left.'

'Keep quiet! I'll massage it for you.'

Wriggling against the rough wood, Kai moved down the cart, grabbed hold of Clod's foot and, tugging off the shoe, began to rub.

'Aagh!' Clod writhed.

'Shhh!' hissed Kai. 'D'you want to get us killed? Bite your hand or something.'

Clod's cries became groans. Finally he tapped Kai on the head. 'Thank you. It's g-g-going. You can stop.'

Kai made his way back up to the front of the cart and peered through the crack.

'Any sign of them m-m-moving?'

'They look like they're really enjoying themselves,' said Kai. 'Joking, smoking and drinking. We could be stuck here all night.'

Clod gave a despairing groan.

'Keep wriggling your toes,' said Kai. 'It'll keep your circulation . . . Oh my God!'

'What!?' said Clod. 'Wh-wh-what is it?'

Kai pressed his eye up close against the crack in the wood. Beyond the militiamen, he could just make out two figures moving like shadows through the dark, creeping around the jeeps. From their size and movements it was clear they weren't adults. 'I'm not sure,' he muttered.

The smaller of the two figures glanced over towards the jeeps. Momentarily illuminated by the headlights, the face was clear across the darkness. Kai gasped. *The girl*. It was her! *It was them!*

26

Bullets Before Breakfast

A bassy, rumbling sound. Deep. Very deep. Deep like the sound that continents make when they shift and rub up against one another. That was the sound Kai could hear. Loud and clear. And he was running through the streets, shouting to people, trying to warn them. 'It's coming! The storm wave is coming! Run for your lives! Run to the high ground.' Some of the people were laughing. Some of them, swayed by his words or the desperation of his voice, took to their heels and followed. He was running. Running fast.

As they charged through the streets, more and more people joined the exodus. Behind him, the sound of running feet grew louder, merging with the deep bass sound of the coming wave. The wave's distant rumble and the thunder of running feet had become one, driving the frantic crowd on. Up through the streets of northern Portobello and on towards the Nebulese border.

A seething, terrified mass, as one, the crowd poured out of Main Street and on towards no-man's-land and the central border crossing. Kai gasped for air; the shouting and running had exhausted him. He was no longer at the front, many had overtaken him. Stopping for breath he glanced back towards the headland. And as he watched, the enormous wave rose up, engulfing Dolphins' Point.

And higher still it grew, as it ploughed on towards Downtown.

A loud explosion spun him round. Screams filled the air. Fleeing Portobellans hurled themselves to the ground. Others froze in terror. 'Keep on the road!' yelled Kai, cupping his hands to his mouth. 'The rest is a minefield. *Keep to the road!!*'

But too many were trying to get to the border. In spite of his warnings, people were spilling off the tarmac, on to the dirt of no-man's-land.

BOOOM! Right in front of his eyes. A mother and child blown into tiny pieces.

BOOOM! Again to the other side. Two boys helping their grandfather.

People scowled at him, elbowed him and shoved him. With a horrible sinking feeling he realized he was standing in their way. He was standing right at the point where everybody was trying to crowd on to the road that led to the border. Apologizing, he began to move again with the flow of people. But the pace was little more than a shuffle, and the deep rumbling sound of the giant wave was growing louder and louder behind them. Downtown now must be under the sea. People kept turning round to check for the wave. It had to be coming up the streets any moment. They wouldn't be high enough till they got through the border gate into Nebula . . .

Suddenly a deafening sound filled his head. DAGGA-DAGGA-DAGGA-DAGGA.

The people in front of him were screaming. They threw themselves to the ground. It was the border guards! As the panic-stricken crowd approached, the Nebulese soldiers were cutting them down with machine guns.

'*No!*' yelled Kai. 'This isn't an attack!' With his hands

142

raised, he stumbled forwards, over bodies of the dead and fallen. 'Don't shoot! *Don't shoot!*'

For a moment there seemed to be a lull in the shooting. Then a deafening roar filled the air around them. Kai and those still standing glanced back to see the wave crashing through the buildings.

As Kai turned and began to run, imploring, towards the Nebulese soldiers, blinding fire flashed from the barrels of their guns. Searing pain stabbed through his chest, his legs crumpled beneath him. Staggering over bodies, with the wave roaring behind him, he collapsed, just metres from the border gate. The Nebulese machine guns blazed white-hot. He hadn't made it.

Bright light – sunshine – streamed in through a hole in the tarpaulin. Squinting against the blinding glare, Kai turned towards the terrible sound in his ear. It was Clod – lying on his back, mouth open, snoring loudly. Kai gave him a shove.

'Ungh!?' Clod jerked up. 'What!? What's h-h-happening?' Spotting Kai, the panic melted from his eyes. 'Oh, thank God! It's you. I was having a bad dream.'

'Me too,' groaned Kai. He threw back the tarpaulin. 'Time to get moving. Today's another market day. The owner of this cart is not going to be happy if they find we've been using it as a bed.' He scrambled to his feet. 'Was there gunfire in your dreams?'

Clod nodded. 'How did you know?'

'I had it in mine too.' Vaulting over the side of the cart, he grinned. 'Probably just the sound of your snoring! Let's hope.'

'Otherwise, a b-b-bad start to the day.'

'It wouldn't be the first time there's been bullets before breakfast in Downtown.'

'Your two f-f-fugitives, maybe?'

Kai nodded. 'Or the freedom fighters . . . the militia . . . or the Nebs . . .'

Clod grunted. 'I hope all last n-n-night's risk-taking to find Mushirah isn't going to be wasted.'

Kai shrugged and stretched. 'Shouldn't you be getting home to the restaurant? If Paps isn't back, you might be opening up on your own.' He offered his hand to help Clod down from the cart.

'What about you?' said Clod.

'I've got a hunch to follow.'

27

Walking Target

Fragments of loosened rock fell away beneath Kai's feet as he scrambled up the scree. The path would have been easier, but on the path he would have been visible from a long way up. A walking target for anyone with a gun. Coming this way, up the bleak east side, he hoped to reach Gorgon's Rest unnoticed.

The climb grew steeper. Now he needed handholds. Several large rocky outcrops blocked his ascent. Though they were wet with spray churned up by Medusa and blown over the headland by the westerlies, he couldn't yet hear her and wouldn't be able to till he neared the top. His left shoulder had only just recovered from the wrench it had suffered when he had tried to shoot the shark. His right wouldn't fully recover from its injury for some time. Jamming the fingers of his left hand into a tight crack in the rock, he tested the pain and the grip. It would have to do. Could he make it to the top one-handed?

Progress proved slow and treacherous. By the time he had cleared the final overhang he was ready for a break. But now he was in full view of Gorgon's Rest and anyone using it as an observation post. Dropping his guard at this stage, even for a moment, was out of the question. Hunched low and stepping lightly, he advanced towards the top, his hand on the *XK7*.

The wind had dropped. Instead of the usual gusts, just an easy breeze was blowing. Nevertheless, the gently rounded summit, overlooked by a steep pinnacle at the end of the ridge, was not a good place to be. The fugitives could be hidden away up there, watching. He was a sitting duck if they had a rifle and telescopic sights. Perhaps they had better things to do. But he wasn't going to wait around to find out.

Kai continued down the other side, towards the old stone plinth where he'd stood with Clod only a few days before. Now the whirlpool's deafening din grew louder with every step. Heading for the cliff's edge, he kept his eyes on the rocks above him.

Of course there was every possibility the fugitives weren't on the headland. It had only been a hunch after all, fuelled by glimpsing them as they crossed the piazza in this direction. They could have doubled back. They could have easily headed off in a different direction without him knowing. But he was here now. Though the headland was vast, if they were here, he was going to find them.

There were not so many places to hide. The other side of the ridge offered shelter from the prevailing winds, but it was just as barren and it was overlooked by the cities. The fugitives wouldn't want that. If they had been out here since the early hours, they'd have had time to explore and investigate all the way to Dolphins' Point. From what he had seen of them so far, they were fast, smart and intrepid. By now they would have assessed the area's potential and decided on one place. It was all guesswork on his part, but so far it had served him very well.

Cut into the side of the cliff, looking out on Medusa, a path descended to a viewing platform half-way down. The path was narrow, steep and in some places dangerously eroded. The very top of it had crumbled away a long time ago and fallen into the sea. Perhaps the plinth had once been a pointer to the path and platform. But because of the shape of the cliffs, without stepping right up to the edge and leaning over, there was nothing to indicate the existence of either.

Those who knew of the viewing platform's existence had theories about how and why it had come into being. Kai believed it was the creation of an ancient Medusa-worshipping culture. Down on that viewing platform, with Medusa roaring at your feet, it was impossible not to feel awe and terror.

With some trepidation, he began to descend. Might the fugitives have found out about the path and platform? In the short time they'd been in Portobello they had survived remarkably well – found somewhere to hide, got themselves guns, escaped him and the militia. Instinct said they would be here. If they weren't already, then it was only a matter of time. The same instinct said it was prudent to draw the *XK7* and release the safety.

With the wind eerily stilled, the fine spray from Medusa hung around the upper cliffs like a mist. In places, the path was badly eroded. The wetness from the mist made it doubly treacherous. Several times already, Kai had been forced to cling to the rock face as he edged his way down.

Peering through the mist he could at last make out the viewing platform below. And there, standing on the edge, pressed against the guard rail, stood a figure. *The boy*. Kai pressed himself against the cliff and watched.

From a distance there was something peculiar about the boy's movements. What was he doing with his arms? And where was the girl? With the roar of Medusa in his ears, Kai edged his way closer, taking his eyes off the platform only to check his footing.

As Kai descended, the mist thinned. Something in front of the boy flashed in the sunlight. Something gossamer thin. What was that? It looked like cable – the strong, ultra-fine kind some of the fishermen used on their nets. And if the boy was pulling on cable, then what was on the other end?

Kai crouched and peered over the edge, down into the sea. *The girl!* She was there, swimming! Right up close to the shore, but there nevertheless. She was attached to the cable at one end, the boy had the other end tied to one of the guard rail posts. Suddenly the strange body movements made sense. He was belaying the cable, reeling it in to take up the slack, as the girl swam in towards the rocks.

The boy cupped a hand to his mouth. 'You were going great!' he yelled. 'Why did you stop?'

The girl kicked and struggled to heave herself up on a rock. Her legs still dangled in the sea. She was clearly exhausted and out of breath. Kai knew she must be. He had tried swimming against that current. Even right in close to the cliffs, Medusa's pull had been overwhelming and he had quickly tired. It took the girl a while to reply. 'It's way too strong!' Her shout sounded spent.

'You give up too easily. Come on! Try again!'

'I'm telling you, Phoenix!'

That was the boy's name then – Phoenix.

He stood silent and irritable. He didn't like her answer. 'Maybe I should have a go.'

The girl shook her head but didn't bother to reply. Or didn't have the strength.

Kai had crept close. But there was still a good thirty

paces to reach the platform and no more cover beyond this last bend in the path. He crouched again, this time aiming the *kombatordnantz*. An accurate shot on the boy would be possible, but with him so close to the edge there was a danger the impact would carry him off the platform.

That he did not want. If he couldn't capture the fugitives alive then at least he wanted their corpses. Otherwise he had nothing to bargain with. To have them hidden away somewhere, trussed up but alive, would be best. Then he could negotiate with Mendel. Make sure he was given what he'd been promised.

The boy Phoenix glanced around nervously, as though he felt the watching eyes. He gave a sharp tug on the cable. 'OK, Phoebe!'

So now Kai knew the girl's name too. As she began to climb she disappeared from sight. Phoenix was braced, belaying the cable to assist her ascent. Preoccupied and, literally, tied up. Perfect! Aiming the *XK7* at the boy's leg, Kai stepped out from behind the rock and moved silently down the path towards him.

He had crossed more than half the distance before Phoenix, sensing his approach, turned. 'You!' His hand edged towards the gun at his hip. A smile twisted his lips. 'Back for more?'

'*Don't!*' snarled Kai. The *XK7*'s laser blazed a red dot on Phoenix's straying hand. But the hand kept moving. Shifting the dot on to the gun, Kai fired.

The impact knocked Phoenix to his knees. The gun lay on the ground near the edge.

'*Phoenix?*' The girl's yell was faint against Medusa's roar.

'Try that again,' said Kai, continuing down the path, 'and I'll blow your hand off.'

28

Raging Torrent

The boy Phoenix cursed and struggled back to his feet. He had let go of the cable when he fell. Now it creaked with the girl's weight against the wooden post. 'You're Portobellan – right?' A sneer curled his lip. 'Some kind of local bounty hunter?'

Ignoring the question, Kai motioned to the gun. 'Kick it over the edge. Make sure you don't hit your friend.'

'Working for Nebula?' Phoenix smiled. 'That must go down well with your fellow citizens.' As his leg swung to kick the pistol, in the same movement he flipped backwards, cartwheeling towards the rear of the platform.

Kai's finger tightened on the trigger.

BLAM! BLAM! BLAM! BLAM! BLAM! Noise filled the air. Bullets ricocheted off the rocks. But the boy had moved with lightning speed. Smoke and dust filled the air, obscuring the back of the platform. Taking a few cautious paces towards where the boy had been standing, Kai crouched and peered. He could see nothing. *Where did he go?*

BOOM-BOOM-BOOM! A trail of explosive rounds ripped through the edge of the platform. Kai was showered with debris as he flattened himself into the rock. The boy had other weapons here!

'*Phoeeeeenix!*'

Instinctively Kai jerked round. It was the girl, down on the cable, alarmed and yelling.

'Big mistake!' A deeper voice.

Kai froze.

'What goes around, comes around!' Phoenix had found his way through the smoke and dust, over to the path. He was aiming a mean-looking short assault rifle right at Kai's face. The lip curled again. 'Not such fun when the gun's aimed at you, huh?' He glared at the *kombatordnantz* in Kai's hands. '*Drop it!*'

It was Kai's turn to obey. Slowly he lowered the barrel of the gun, so it pointed towards the ground. His mind was racing. He had no doubt Phoenix would shoot him. But to just give up his gun . . .

Phoenix scowled. 'No funny business!'

Kai let go of the *XK7*. It clattered to the ground.

'Good,' said Phoenix. 'Now step away from it.' He gestured with his gun towards the far end of the platform.

With one eye on Phoenix's trigger finger, Kai did as he was told.

'*Phoenix?*' The girl's yell floated up from the cliff below. Her voice was faint against the sea's roar – she was still some way down. 'Are you OK?'

'Yeah.' Anxiously watching Kai, Phoenix took a couple of steps towards the edge. 'How you doing?' He leant a little. 'Sorry I had to abandon the cable. I'm a little busy right now. Can you make it up here on your own?'

There was no response.

With the force of the wind and the loudness of Medusa, Kai figured there was a good chance the girl on the cliff couldn't hear a word her friend was saying. But no one was asking for his opinion.

Phoenix took another cautious step towards the edge.

151

'Phoebe?' Suddenly he was waving his arms – not waving to the girl, but in the uncontrolled fashion of someone losing their balance. Kai saw rock crumbling away beneath the boy's feet. BOOM-BOOM-BOOM! Flames flashed from the barrel of the gun. Diving sideways to avoid the bullets, Kai charged low towards the flailing figure.

As boy and blazing gun slid beneath the rail and vanished over the platform's collapsing edge, Kai flung himself, arms outstretched, grabbing blindly. Catching hold of something, instinctively he wrapped his legs round a guard rail post.

He was clutching Phoenix's ankle.

'Eeeagh!' Phoenix's body crunched against the cliff.

'Aaaaagh!' Pain seared through Kai's wound as his shoulders were wrenched by the boy's weight. Below him the gun clattered down the cliff, narrowly missing the climbing girl.

'*Phoenix!*' The girl screamed as she looked up.

Phoenix groaned, hawked and spat blood. 'I think I broke my nose.' His laugh was manic. 'But apart from that . . .' He jerked, doing a half sit-up to peer up at Kai. A bloody grin. 'How you doin'?'

Kai could feel himself being dragged away from the post. His grip wasn't a match for the boy's weight. 'Don't move like that,' he gasped. 'You're too heavy. I can't hold you.'

'Poor puny Portobellan!' Phoenix shook with laughter. 'Better hang on, Mr Bounty Hunter, or you're going to lose your reward!'

Kai tried to tighten his grip on the post but it was no use – like everything else it was wet from the seaspray. He was slipping.

'*Phoenix!*' There was anger in the girl's voice. 'Stop it!'

Phoenix laughed even harder.

'What's wrong with you?' Phoebe was climbing fast. 'It's *your* life he's trying to save!'

'I don't think so,' said Phoenix. 'This boy's trying to save something for himself.'

'Reach up!' urged Kai. 'Slowly. See if you can grab my hands.' His own body was being pulled over the edge – didn't the boy realize that?

'Funny guy!' Phoenix laughed again, thrashing wildly as he did so. 'You think I'm going to *fall* for that!'

'*Phoenix!*' The girl was imploring.

'No way!' yelled Phoenix. He grinned up at Kai. 'I'm not giving myself up to you! To be handed over like some escaped zoo animal? Uh-uuuh! I've tasted liberty! And I like it!' He kicked upwards with his free foot.

Kai's fingers stung with pain, but still he clung tight with his remaining hand. The boy was trying to break his grip! The ankle was slipping. He himself was half over the edge . . .

'*Phoenix!*'

Phoenix wriggled and kicked.

Kai could hold on no longer. His grip was breaking. Broken.

'See you in the land of the freeeeeeeeeeee!' Arms outstretched, dropping past Phoebe, Phoenix fell, laughing, headlong towards the water.

Kai watched, stunned. Avoiding all rocks and protrusions, the boy hit the ocean in a practically perfect dive. Hardly a splash.

'*Phoenix.*' Still clinging to the cable, the girl glanced up.

'Hang on!' yelled Kai. 'I can help you.'

The girl looked doubtful. She turned to glance down at the ocean. There was no sign of the boy in the water.

When she looked up again her expression had changed. She climbed in a hurry, reaching up when she was near.

Kai grabbed her hand and pulled her up over the side.

'Can you see him?' The girl looked and sounded shaken.

Kai peered down into the sea. 'Hey, yeah! I see him!' He pointed. 'There! Between the outer rim of Medusa and the cliff. He's trying to swim towards the open ocean.'

Pressing herself flat against the rock beside him, the girl stretched out over the edge and peered. 'Oh my God! I see him!' She turned, her face drawn. 'He's being dragged backwards!'

Kai nodded. 'The current's way too strong . . .'

As they watched, the small figure thrashing against the waves was being pulled backwards towards Medusa's foaming outer wall with gathering speed. He crashed through this barrier like a bullet, still travelling backwards. He was visible fleetingly in the darker water of the vast inner walls, still slashing at the water with his arms, still struggling against overwhelming force. Then suddenly he was gone, lost in the raging torrent, as it whirled and drained inevitably towards the gaping centre.

Kai was so transfixed, it was several moments before he noticed the girl was gone from beside him. How long had he been staring at Medusa, waiting in vain for some glimmer of hope that the boy Phoenix had survived? Alerted by a sound, he jerked round. The girl was standing a short distance up the path.

'Sorry,' she said. 'I have to do this.' Crouching, she placed something small on the ground, turned and hurried off towards the top.

Before Kai could get to his feet the grenade exploded.

29

Taking Stock

Grey sludge. Everywhere. When Kai opened his eyes, that was all he could see. His face was lying in the stuff. His body felt stiff, like he had been lying there for some time. His head hurt.

Then he remembered – the blast from the grenade! He had been trying to get to his feet. It had knocked him back down. The whole viewing platform had been showered with rock and debris. Something must have struck his skull. Everything else was a blank.

He moved his arm. Flexed his fingers. Slowly his hand edged up towards the back of his head, where the pain was centred. He touched stickiness. But then everything was sticky – the clouds of dust from the blast had mixed with the seaspray and turned to mud. He dabbed at the pain and brought his hand round to look. *Blood!*

Slowly, gingerly, he raised himself up on to his knees. A little rubbing took away some of the stiffness. His head throbbed. The bleeding had stopped, but he felt dizzy and weak. He looked around. The grenade had blown a big chunk out of the cliff path. Unless he could find some way past the gaping hole, he was trapped.

He stared down at roaring Medusa, replaying in his mind's eye the events that had preceded the grenade. The Neb boy Phoenix had been a strong swimmer. Courageous too. But the she-monster had sucked him in and swallowed him like a fly. And what happened down there?

Kai's eyes strained to pierce the dark obscurity at the whirlpool's centre. From the first time he set eyes on Medusa, he had always wanted to know if someone who, like him, could hold their breath for a long, long time were to be sucked down inside the whirlpool, could they survive? They would be dragged right down to the very heart of the beast and then what? Would the currents along the bottom whisk them out to the open ocean? Or would they be dragged back into the edges of the vortex to be sucked down again, and again, and again in a never-ending cycle?

Kai felt a perverse pang of envy. The fugitives could hold their breath a long time. Probably longer than him. Maybe Phoenix was still holding his now? Unlikely. But one way or the other, somewhere out there, Phoenix had all the answers.

Medusa was at her most powerful at low tide – something to do with the shape of the rocks on the ocean bed beneath her. She had grown in size and strength while Kai had been unconscious. The tide was on its way out.

Kai let his gaze drift out over the ocean, towards the horizon. He could just sit here and wait for the wave. *It was coming*. This was the ideal place on the headland to catch the rebound. He had given it a great deal of thought since the deep groaning noises started, all those weeks back. He would make his escape while Medusa was flooded out and powerless.

This was the place he'd selected. That was why he'd expected the fugitives to be here. They were smart like him. Thought the same way. They had worked out all the possibilities. Come up with the same result.

And when would the wave come? Soon, he was certain. The groans had been getting closer together and louder. The sign. But if he sat here and waited he might grow too weak. Lack of food. He would need all his strength and stamina to reach even the nearest of the small islands.

There was another problem too. Here, half-way down the side of the cliff, there was a good chance he would be swept away by the storm wave's initial rush. If this wave was as high as the one he remembered, as high as the one in his nightmares, then he wouldn't stand a chance.

And there was still the opportunity to earn an easier escape. He had fulfilled one half of the deal with the SIA man, Mendel. One fugitive was dead.

Time to go after the second.

30

Black Widow

Kai stared up at the cliff face. There had to be a way round the gap in the path. The rocks were sheer, but hadn't the girl climbed right up to the platform from the sea? She had used the cable. It was still attached to the post, maybe there was a way he could use it too.

But no. The cable was only attached to the platform, not to anything above. He couldn't use it to swing across the gap. Kai wound the cable round his arm, reeling it in to see how much there was. If he tied himself to a short length, that would at least give the security of knowing he wouldn't drop so far if he fell. He smiled to himself. The fall would still probably kill him!

He rubbed the back of his neck. The ache in his head seemed to be getting worse. He could hear a throbbing now too. And it was growing louder, in waves. So loud, in fact, that his whole body was beginning to quake. He clutched himself. The waves of throbbing weren't inside his head at all, they were drowning out Medusa! They sounded like . . .

As he spun round, a wall of air and noise knocked him off his feet. There, staring him in the face, like some giant, mutant spider on invisible thread, hovered a helicopter gunship. One of the infamous Nebulese Black Widows. A shiver ran down his spine. *The ultimate killer*. And all of its awesome firepower was aimed right at *him*.

He squinted against the down-draught from the blades. Two people in the cockpit wore black shiny helmets. The third had a face he recognized.

'*We were worried about you!*' The voice, distorted by noise and amplification, was Mendel's. '*Your transmitter showed you stationary for too long. Good to see you're still alive!*' One of the helmeted figures made a sign to Mendel. '*Stay where you are,*' said Mendel's amplified voice. '*We can't get in any closer. We'll have to take her up above the cliff then winch you on board.*'

Kai gave the thumbs-up signal.

With scarcely a wobble, the gunship began to rise. Up, up, up. Magnificent, controlled and dignified. Kai watched it go. When it reached the top, a figure appeared from a hatch in the belly and began a rapid descent. Within seconds a Nebulese marine was on the platform in front of him, strapping him into a harness and signalling to the winchman to reel them both up.

As the gunship rose and twisted away from the cliff, Kai was snatched up and whisked off in the arms of the marine. His cheeks stretched back in a grin of pure exhilaration. Speed rush.

Looking down as they soared out over swirling Medusa, Kai thought of ospreys. He was up in their world now. This was what it was like. This must be how they saw things.

When at last he put his feet down inside the gunship, Kai felt giddy from so much sensation. The noise was incredible. Strong hands grabbed him and helped him out of his harness. Another marine took his arm and led him towards the front of the helicopter.

On the other side of the narrow opening, Mendel greeted him and pointed towards a seat. 'Strap yourself in. It might get a bit bumpy. We'll be arriving in a few moments.'

Kai obeyed. 'Arriving where?'

'You'll see.'

As well as the view through the windows, there was a screen displaying the ground directly below. Kai had never been in the air before, except for those few fleeting seconds when he took dives off the headland. Now, as the gunship rose up, what he saw left him stunned.

Columns of thick dark smoke rose up into the sky. Buildings were blazing in Downtown. A boat was in flames and much of the harbour was hidden beneath a thick pall. People no bigger than ants scattered and ran as other Black Widow gunships swooped low, guns flashing. Hovering above the main piazza, two more of the beasts launched double rocket volleys.

Kai felt his stomach knot and tighten. It wasn't vertigo, but a whole welter of feelings rushing up. He recognized the street where several buildings had just burst into flames spewing fragments skywards. It was the street he and Clod had visited the other night. Where the PFF had one of their safe houses.

Not any more.

They moved swiftly across the city towards the gleaming offices of NebEx, NebBank and NebTech. There was smoke, Kai noticed, billowing from the base of the NebEx complex. The freedom fighters, it appeared, had struck back at their sworn enemies. Mendel tapped the pilot on the arm and gestured. The pilot nodded and the gunship began a gentle descent down to the roof of the NebTech tower.

31

Status Report

Jaws clenched, Kai stood by the window gazing out on the city, fifty storeys below. 'Your boys seem to be having a fairly easy time of it down there.' There was more than a hint of a sneer in his voice. 'I'd say it was quite a one-sided battle.'

They were in the NebTech penthouse boardroom. Mendel was seated in a plush leather chair. 'I agree.' He rested his elbows on the enormous walnut table. 'The military, however, are not under my command.'

'But you are Nebulese,' said Kai.

'You could be too,' said Mendel. 'All the advantages of Nebulese citizenship could be yours. Which brings me to the point – our fugitives, may I have a status report?'

Kai pushed unease and irritation to one side. 'The boy is dead. I aim to capture the girl alive. Soon, hopefully.'

'Dead or alive doesn't matter,' said Mendel. 'But soon rather than later does.' He gestured towards the scene ouside the window. 'Because of that, I'm afraid our deadline's been brought forwards.' He glanced at his watch. 'You've got until midnight.'

'*Tonight!?*'

Mendel nodded. 'After that the deal is off. I have to brief the president tomorrow.'

They had changed the rules. He had known they'd cheat him all along. 'And then what? Nebula declares war?'

Mendel shrugged. 'What about the dead boy? Did you bring proof?'

'Take it from me,' said Kai. 'He's dead.'

Mendel stiffened. 'No evidence?'

'What did you expect? He dropped from a cliff, into the whirlpool.' Kai scowled. 'I did my best to hold on to him.'

'Of course.'

Hold on to the anger too. He jerked his head sideways, first one way then the other, cracking the vertebrae in his neck. He was armed. At no point had anyone searched him. He had the *XK7*. And now, all of a sudden, the angry part of him wanted to whip it out and blow Mendel's face off. With his own gun. Splatter him across the immaculate NebTech boardroom. 'It's been a tough day. I'm exhausted. And I think I'm wasting my time.'

'You're not.' Mendel looked away, unable to hold Kai's intense glare. 'It's just . . .' His brow furrowed. 'Having no no evidence, no corpse, is a little awkward. That's all.'

'Medusa will hold a person for hours,' said Kai. 'Maybe forever. I watched the whirlpool and the area around it for a long time. There was no sign.'

'Good.' Mendel nodded. 'Then I think, under the circumstances, we can assume he is dead.'

'He counts?'

'He does.' Mendel got to his feet. 'Now . . . I'm afraid with all this going on,' he gestured towards the gun battle outside, 'I have pressing matters to attend to. I will be at the north lighthouse at midnight. If you could bring me the girl?'

32

Charred and Broken Bodies

The fighting was over. People were out in the streets in large numbers. Kai was walking briskly, too briskly, making his way back towards Downtown. Each time he was jostled or bumped, he grunted or snapped; each time it fed his anger. He was in a hurry. There was little time left. And he was in a bad mood. Stormy.

He didn't trust Mendel. He had never trusted anyone he did business with, least of all Paps. But there was a difference. If Mendel betrayed him there was little he could do about it.

Kai found himself pushing against a sea of angry chanting people. For a moment he was back in the nightmare of the night before, the feelings of helpless frustration, the swelling panic. It had become a tradition, following Nebulese raids, for the corpses of fresh victims to be carried above the heads of the crowd, all the way to no-man's-land and the border. The men grim-faced, the women wailing and shedding tears, they paraded their slain loved ones before the enemy.

'Look!' they yelled. 'See the work of your malevolent Black Widows!'

'These charred and broken bodies. These bloodied corpses. These are what your gunships have left us with!'

'This is the result of your bloody reprisals!'

'The blood of our mothers, wives, daughters . . .'

'The blood of our fathers, husbands, sons . . .'

'The blood of innocent children is on *your* hands!'

More young Portobellans would be recruited by the PFF. More raids would be launched against Nebulese targets. And in turn, there would be more doubly deadly retaliation.

A bloody, self-perpetuating cycle. A vicious circle. Except – maybe this time it was all about to end. Mendel had implied that if his fugitive problem wasn't dealt with by midnight, his president had plans. Would Nebula really go so far as to raze Portobello to the ground? Would they annihilate the whole city?

Only if the wave didn't first.

Kai entered the large piazza, heading for the Green Star Noodle Bar. No market today. Another crowd. This one more strident and defiant than those he had passed in the streets. The thousands here had been whipped up to fever pitch by a small, vociferous group of PFF fighters. Dressed in their uniforms, some of them adorned with blood-red *martyr* headbands, the PFF chanted slogans of resistance from a platform in the centre of the square.

The people of Portobello would triumph over their oppressors. The Nebulese wanted to grind them down and drive them into the sea, but the spirit of the Portobellan people was uncrushable. Portobello may have been bent double like a sapling under the force of the massive Nebulese army, but she would spring back. The Almighty was on their side. Victory was assured.

A sudden burst of automatic gunfire crackled above the crowd. People ducked, heads jerked, eyes instinctively darted heavenwards. But this was not another attack. No helicopter gunships hung in the sky. It was a phalanx of

PFF gunmen entering the square, guns in the air. A military salute, heralding a procession of corpses. As the crowd's roar joined the din of gunfire, newly martyred PFF fighters, carried by friends, family and comrades-in-arms, floated their way over heads into the piazza.

And the corpses kept coming. As each dead fighter arrived at the platform their name was announced to the crowd. Taking up the name, the crowd chanted ritual praise and, led by those on the platform, proclaimed the *martyr* status of the dead fighter.

Being swallowed up by a PFF rally had done little for Kai's irritability. Time was running out. The crowd was densely packed and its mood was ugly. This was not the occasion for pushing and barging. After several frustrated attempts to move towards the Green Star Noodle Bar, he resigned himself to going with the flow. Everyone was moving in the same direction with the same purpose. Whether he liked it or not, he was heading for the platform.

What was he going to do when he got free of the crowd, anyway? With just a few hours to track down the girl, what chance did he have? What did he have to go on? Nothing.

Wrapped in the PFF flag and adorned with flowers, the bodies of the fallen had been laid side by side around the base of the platform so they could be viewed. As Kai shuffled with the crowd past the first few, all thoughts of hunting fugitives evaporated. Here were faces he recognized. Faces of PFF fighters from the house he and Clod had visited just a few nights before. Had Mushirah managed to deliver her warning? Had it been heeded? A heavy sense of dread sank over him as he approached the end of the line.

Then suddenly it was there. The face he did not want to see.

Topaz.

Her eyes were closed as though merely sleeping, but her skin had paled and her cheeks looked slightly sunken. Somebody had taken the time to comb and style her hair. They had also wiped away the blood and as much as possible cleaned up the fatal head wound. With the life drained out of her, she looked familiar but different.

He had never seen Topaz sleeping, he realized. Her eyes were such a striking part of her that with them closed her face looked serene but depleted. Her nose was strong, her mouth full-lipped. Had he never noticed before? These beautiful features seemed somehow isolated and diminished now the sparkle that had brought them together was gone.

Placing a silver teapot, two glasses and a bowl of rock sugar on the table, Clod sat. 'You look like a g-g-ghost.'

Kai gave a feeble nod. He felt sick. Everyone in Downtown was used to death. He, presumably, more than most. After all, it had been one of his trades. But people dealt with it by keeping it distant or at least at arm's length.

Moving on, finally, from the face of dead Topaz, he had been passed by another procession. Winding round the outside of the piazza, the mourners had been carrying an old woman's corpse raised up on their shoulders. Another innocent victim of the reprisals. As the procession had drawn closer, he had recognized the face and found himself shaking. *Mushirah*. Not wrapped in a PFF flag, but adorned with flowers and laid out on a door. The door perhaps of the very house she had been visiting – the PFF safe house.

'Bad d-d-day?'

'One corpse after another.'

Clod frowned. 'Not your fugitives, I s-s-suppose, or you'd be looking more cheerful.'

Kai shook his head. Then he remembered. 'One of them died too.'

'*Ah!* One down, one to g-g-go, then?'

Kai gave a vague shrug. He had lost his focus. There was a fast approaching deadline and he was doing nothing.

The smell of fresh peppermint filled the air as Clod poured tea. 'Paps still hasn't c-come home,' he said. 'I suppose he might have b-b-been injured in the raid. But knowing him, he's just b-b-busy with business. I've been m-managing fine without him so far.'

Kai nodded.

'I quite enjoy the shopping and c-cooking. As you and I got up at such an early hour this morning, I was able to get d-d-down to the fish market before anyone else. I got all the b-best fish.' Clod dropped a large lump of rock sugar into Kai's glass and stirred – a gesture of friendship. 'Actually, I overheard this convers-s-sation which I thought m-m-might interest you.' He passed the glass to Kai. 'Probably not?'

'No, go on, please. I'm listening.' Sipping his tea, Kai forced himself to concentrate.

'I overheard these two f-f-fishermen talking about an old c-c-colleague. They were saying how he had gone m-missing a few days before, but his b-b-boat was still moored up.'

The strong sweet taste of fresh peppermint was revitalizing. Kai felt his mind reaching back, making connections. There had been a particular smell he had noticed as he'd tried to hold on to the fugitive boy's legs. A strong and distinctly fishy smell, coming off his boots . . .

167

'I'm sure there's a qu-qu-quite ordinary explanation – the fisherman probably got drunk somewhere, or m-m-met a woman.' Clod shrugged. 'It just struck me that this disap-p-pearance happened about the same time your t-t-two fugitives would have been l-l-looking for somewhere to stay.'

'*Which boat!?*' Jumping up, Kai dragged Clod from his seat. 'This is *very* important. How can we find it? Would you recognize the fishermen?'

Clod gawped, stunned by Kai's sudden outburst of enthusiasm. 'A-a-actually, I know exactly where to f-f-find it.'

33

Fish and Flies

Phoebe had been living with the buzz of flies and the stench of rotting fish for so long now she no longer noticed it. Occasionally her hand made a spasmodic twitch like the tail on a beast of burden, but it was an unconscious reaction she barely noticed. She sat alone in the darkening cabin, with nothing but her thoughts.

It had all gone so wrong. Lying in her nice clean bed, in her nice clean room, in her nice clean laboratory or whatever you called that place, she'd imagined things working out quite differently. She'd had time to spend dreaming about what escape would be like and how things might turn out. Never once had she come close.

For starters, Portobello was essentially a prison too. There was nowhere to run. That had thrown her and Phoenix completely. The speed with which the Nebulese authorities had found a Portobellan to hunt down the two of them had been another shock. The boy was young like them. And immediately seemed to be a match for them – adept underwater, fast, agile and stealthy. There had been no time for her and Phoenix to adjust. They were out in the real world. They were aliens. And straight away they had been on the run.

Poor Phoenix. That final image – him struggling with all his might against the raging torrent, being dragged backwards down into the spiralling waters – had replayed itself again and again in her head. In her dreams, during those rare moments when she had managed sleep, she saw his pale body suspended in a blue-green watery limbo, his lips, muted by the ocean's depths, making the same shapes over and over. Her brother. Her blood. Her twin.

How poorly, it turned out, she had known him. All their lives they had lived in such close proximity. Yet almost as soon as they crossed that border, Phoenix had become a different, quite frightening, creature.

Had she missed the signs that had been there all along? Either way, it was too late now. He was gone. And she was on her own. Alone in a world that terrified her.

The strange thing was, the one person she did feel any kind of connection to was the boy. The fascinating, dangerous boy. He had tried to save Phoenix, hadn't he? Not kill him. There was something about his face, something about him which she just couldn't shake off.

The first time she'd spotted him, swimming in the sea just off the safe beach, he'd been down at dark green depths unmodifieds weren't supposed to be able to reach. She and Phoenix had argued about it. Phoenix had insisted she must have imagined what she had seen, or there was some other explanation. He hadn't been interested in hearing her theory. And then at the fish stall she had noticed the long fingers. Big hands.

Her peculiar feelings about the boy had refused to go away. She had thought about him a lot since that first encounter. And the more she thought about him, the more she felt certain she knew who he was. It all made sense.

Cries of gulls filled the air. The sun was down and light was beginning to drain from the flaming sky. Kai stooped, snatched up a shell from the cobbles and hurled it up over the masts and out across the harbour. There was no sign of the burning boat he had earlier seen from the air. Perhaps it had sunk? On the harbourside, fishermen were busy as usual, readying their nets for the evening's tide and grumbling about the weather. They knew the signs. A big storm was brewing.

'That's the one.' Clod pointed and panted as he caught up.

Kai peered. The little green-and-red fishing boat was moored just a short distance away, the very furthest end of the fleet. A perfect hiding place. He felt deeply uneasy. 'It could simply be that the old fisherman's sick.'

'Or aw-w-way somewhere,' said Clod. 'The men I overh-h-heard didn't seem so concerned. Just surprised he'd not t-t-told anyone.'

'Either way,' said Kai, 'it would make a perfect place for someone to hide. Thanks for the tip-off.'

Clod grinned nervously. 'You can owe me.'

Phoebe lay supine on the wooden bench seat, breathing long and slow, smooth and even. She had lain like this for some time, still and silent, lulled into a state of deepest thought by the rhythm of the boat as it gently rocked on the waves.

But suddenly she was alert and sitting bolt upright. Something had startled her, something had shaken her from her reverie. *What was it?*

Swivelling her legs round to the floor, she crouched and listened. It wasn't a sound that had startled her. No. Her body had sensed a change in the rhythm of the boat's rocking. The rhythm had altered just ever so slightly. Now it was returning again to its regular pattern. *Had someone stepped on board?*

The creaking of timber and rope – were there any changes there? Any out of the ordinary sounds that might indicate the movement of someone on deck? She held her breath and listened.

Light and colour were leaching rapidly from the sky; it would soon be dark, but Kai still kept the *XK7* hidden in case of watchful eyes. As he stepped lightly on to the deck of the little boat, his index finger stroked the trigger for reassurance. Had the boat dipped a little with his weight? He didn't think so. Over on the jetty Clod was giving him an encouraging thumbs-up.

Not moving for a few moments, Kai listened to the sounds of the boat and allowed himself to grow used to its rhythm. A storm was brewing again, the signs were there; dark clouds had smothered the sunset and now the sea was growing restless. This one was could be a cracker when it broke. By the morning maybe? The storm to end all storms.

Creeping on his toes to the cabin door, Kai pressed an ear to the painted wood. He could hear something, a bottle perhaps, rolling back and forth on the wooden floor, in time to the movement of the waves. Other sounds too – the grumbles and groans of an old boat, but nothing he could identify as human. He reached for the handle on the door.

Someone was up there. There was no doubt in Phoebe's mind. Whoever it was, they had been creeping around on deck. Maybe it was the fisherman who owned the boat? She grabbed the assault rifle which Phoenix had left. *Hide it.*

In the floor there was a trapdoor to the hold. It was

172

empty, Phoenix had said, but for some rotting fish, hence the smell and the flies. Not a pleasant prospect, but she would take the gun and climb in there.

Pulling back the rug, she silently slid the bolt and dug her fingers into the crack. As she lifted the trapdoor a stench wafted up from the hold, so strong it knocked her breath clean away. She clutched her mouth, the taste of vomit rising in her throat. Her knees wanted to buckle. But even in the half-light she could see the cabin door handle moving. Someone was out there and about to come in. Crouching at the trapdoor's edge, she extended one foot into the darkness.

'*Aaaaaaaaaaaaaaaaaaaaaagh!*'

It was more scream of terror than yell of aggression. Piercingly loud, and pained enough to curdle blood, it burst its way from the belly of the boat. With his hand on the cabin door handle, Kai's heart missed a beat and he froze.

Suddenly he was yanking at the handle, tugging the door open and thundering down the steps into the darkness. The screaming doubled in loudness and an odour, the most overpowering stench he had ever encountered, hit him like a punch on the nose.

Crouched by a hole in the floor, a figure turned at the sound of his approach. *The Girl.* Clutching herself, eyes and mouth wide with terror, it was she who was doing the screaming.

Hurling himself, Kai knocked the girl to the floor with the force of his body and clamped a hand over her mouth. The two of them rolled. Beneath him the girl twisted and struggled with a desperate energy. Her terrified eyes flitted again and again to the square hole in the floor. Her shrieking, though muffled, grew louder.

173

'*Shhh!*' hissed Kai.

But the girl wasn't listening. She writhed like a mad thing and bit him.

'*Shhh!*' Kai struggled to keep his hand pressed against her mouth and contain her wild movements. 'Please! You'll alert the militia. I'm not going to hurt you!'

His words had no effect. The girl was too terrified to listen. What had so shaken her? Using all his weight to restrain her, Kai leant over towards the trapdoor and peered down into the hold.

34

Cinderella's Slipper

The harbour was almost empty. All but a few boats had headed out to sea for the night's fishing. A strong breeze was up and even inside the shelter of the harbour walls waves were developing a sizeable swell. Kai and Clod sat on the jetty's edge, the girl sandwiched tightly between them.

'I was w-w-worried,' said Clod. 'She's got powerful lungs! I thought she'd br-br-bring the whole of Downtown running. Some of the f-f-fishermen at least.' He glanced towards the boat. 'Can I take a look at the b-b-b . . .' He clenched his fists. 'B-b-b . . .'

'Body?' said Kai. 'A fully grown man, crawling with maggots? Believe me . . .' He shook his head. 'You do not want to see.'

The girl shuddered miserably.

'Didn't know he was down there, huh?'

She shook her head and bit a knuckle.

What should he do with her?

Clod sniffed the air, frowned, glanced at the girl and shrugged.

'Wondering what the smell is?' She turned, her eyes narrow dagger slits. 'Your friend *threw up* on me,' she snapped. She scowled, first at Clod then at Kai, wiping her hands on her thighs.

Clod twitched.

Grateful for the shelter of the dark, Kai bowed his head. The girl had a sharp tongue. 'At least,' he muttered, 'it stopped you screaming.'

She stiffened.

He . . . liked her.

'If you don't need me,' Clod bobbed his head as he tried to look past the girl towards Kai, 'I th-th-think I ought to be getting b-b-back to the restaurant.'

Kai nodded. 'I've got stuff to sort out yet tonight.' His tone was sombre. 'I'll pass by tomorrow.'

With a nod Clod scrambled to his feet and hobbled off into the darkness.

Kai watched the lights of two fishing boats as they entered the harbour and made their way back to their moorings. The fishermen had not been gone long, certainly not long enough to have cast their nets and made a catch. And already they were giving up for the night. A bad sign.

Next to him Phoebe shifted her position, swinging her legs around and letting them, like his, dangle over the water. 'That's pretty much everything,' she said. 'The short version.'

She had left him stranded out on the cliff. As good as dead maybe, if Mendel hadn't come searching for him. But she hadn't killed him when she'd had the chance. He had always known she wasn't someone he would kill. But could he still hand her over?

More lights bobbed through the harbour entrance from the darkness beyond. Kai found his gaze drawn. At first the boats had drifted home in ones and twos. Now the remainder of the fleet was traipsing back in an almost continuous stream. Fishermen did not abandon a night's catch lightly. Out there on the open sea it must be rough. Was a major storm brewing?

Phoebe shifted again. Leaning forwards, she reached down to her ankles and made a tutting noise. 'It's too tight.' Her face pleaded. 'It's chafing.' She peered into his eyes. 'I'm not going to run away.'

Kai said nothing. He'd been worried not so much that she might *run* away, but that she might slip into the dark water and vanish. Like the last time. He'd never met anyone who could match him for speed in the water. No one had ever come near. He had her now, and he was going to hang on to her till he'd decided what to do. Binding her ankles had been a sensible precaution. And tethering her to the steps.

She was still staring at him. Waiting for a response. 'Trying to decide whether to shoot me? Or hand me over?'

Kai shrugged.

Phoebe sighed. 'Anyone ever tell you that you talk too much?'

'No.'

'Really.' Flat. 'Now why aren't I surprised?'

Kai smiled to himself. *Full of fight.* In spite of his best efforts to see her as an object, he was failing. He was in control but somehow she was winning.

'You vomit on me . . .' said Phoebe. 'You tie me up and tie me down. All very exciting! You get me to tell you about myself. After which you sit, staring blankly into the darkness, saying nothing.'

She cocked her head, examining his expression. 'Perhaps you're planning to bore me to death?' Closer. 'Even if you do intend some horrible end for me, couldn't you at least say something about yourself first? I don't even know your name.'

'Kai.'

Phoebe tried out the sound and smiled. 'I like that. Is it traditional Portobellan?'

Kai shook his head.

'Well thank you for sharing that with me. Anything else, Mr Forthcoming? How about if I ask you some questions?'

The more she looked at him, spoke to him, thought about it, the more she felt certain he was who she suspected. 'Your mother died when you were young. You grew up fending for yourself. And you are the fastest and strongest swimmer in the whole of Portobello . . .'

Kai nodded grumpily. Divulging even the smallest snippet about himself had left him uncomfortable.

'Oh, yes!' said Phoebe, remembering. 'But not many people swim in this city because there's only one beach and, in spite of the nets, people are afraid of the sharks?'

'Correct.'

She had only ever heard rumours, stories from staff, well, really one member of staff in particular. But if there was a kernel of truth in them, this boy Kai fitted the story exactly. Hadn't she sensed it that very first time? Hadn't she known? It was like Cinderella and her slipper. But how could she show him, how could she prove it to him, how could she get him to try the slipper on?

It had started to rain again. Phoebe wiped her face. It was refreshing. If her hunch was right then Kai would be enjoying the damp on his skin just as much as she was. But he wouldn't know that about her. 'Couldn't we go somewhere more sheltered?' She nodded towards the wharves. 'Just out of the rain. It's getting pretty wet.' She could just make out his scowl in the darkness.

'OK, then.' He hesitated. 'We'll give it a try.' He gestured. 'Raise your feet.'

Lifting her legs, Phoebe positioned her feet on the jetty between them.

He quickly undid the rope tethering her to the steps. But as he started on the one which bound her ankles together, he faltered.

'Second thoughts?' Phoebe held her wrists out together. 'You can bind my arms if that'll make you any feel better. I'm not going anywhere. Where could I go *to*?' She pulled at the rope, showing how tight it was. 'If you just loosen it enough so I can shuffle. It's dark, no one's going to see.'

For the briefest of moments, their hands touched in blackness.

Phoebe froze, startled by the shiver that rippled through her body. Her laugh sounded nervous. 'A girl with shackled feet – it's not as though anyone in this barbaric town would bat an eyelid.'

'I was going to take you to a bar,' said Kai. 'It's getting cold now too.'

'In that case,' said Phoebe, 'perhaps you should take the rope off completely.'

He looked at her. Nodded. 'OK.'

In spite of the dark and wet he quickly had the knot undone.

Phoebe got to her feet with deliberate slowness, hoping to reassure him there would be no sudden moves. But just as she straightened and stretched, it happened. The strange noises began. The groaning, grumbling sounds from the bowels of the world. She trembled. It had that effect every time. It was powerful. It was easy to see why it had so disturbed the little ones. Though she knew it was seismic in origin, it still made her shake.

At first she hadn't noticed, because she'd been so used to having Phoenix and took it for granted that he could hear everything she could. But suddenly she realized Kai was hearing it – he had turned pale; he was shaking too. He walked off a short distance, hoping, she supposed, to conceal his disquiet. The noise this time was louder and deeper than on any previous occasion. It didn't stop.

'Kai.' Phoebe touched his hand.

He flinched and jerked round.

Even in the dark she could see the terror in his face.

Pushing away her own fear, she summoned a smile. 'You hear it too, don't you?'

'*You* hear it?'

Phoebe nodded. 'We're the only ones.'

Kai frowned. 'We?'

'I know who you really are.'

35

Guinea Pigs Don't Have Parents

From beneath his hood Kai glanced at the men gathered round the next table. Old Neptune regulars. He recognized some of them from the other night's session. Right now he wanted to be incognito.

'Don't worry,' said Phoebe, 'they're all too busy laughing and chatting to be eavesdropping.'

'OK . . .' Kai sipped his drink. 'So I hear what you hear. I have big hands. I can swim far faster than any Portobellan and hold my breath underwater for what by Portobellan standards seems a very long time. But I practise.'

'How long can you hold it?'

'Seven minutes.'

'*Seven!*?' Phoebe's eyes widened with astonishment.

'Only if I'm lying still,' said Kai. 'Less if I'm swimming.'

'That's still spectacular. The most I've ever managed is less than six. Nearer five, if I'm swimming. And we trained daily.'

'Still doesn't prove anything.'

'Do you know what a library is?'

'Duh?' Kai scowled, indignant. 'Of course!'

Phoebe shrugged. 'I'm not to know. I haven't spotted one since I arrived in this place. Plenty of people in Portobello carry guns. No one carries books.'

'We have libraries,' said Kai. 'Your point is?'

181

'I used to spend a lot of time in the library before I ran away from the NebTech complex. Frankly, it was the best thing about the place. And the one member of staff I became really close to was a librarian. I used to help her out when the library was closed. I was her unofficial assistant. She and I used to have long discussions while restocking the shelves.'

'I don't see what this has to do with me. With who I am.'

'You're too impatient.' Phoebe narrowed her eyes. 'I can see you've never read a good story.'

'Is this going anywhere? I like stories with a point.'

Phoebe scowled. 'Do you know what an affair is?'

Kai groaned. 'Of course!'

'Well my librarian friend was having one with Dr Kravitz.'

Kai drummed his fingers on the table. This was a girls' story.

'Dr Kravitz,' said Phoebe, 'is a genius. He's the brains behind the whole second generation project.'

'He created all you . . .' Kai searched for the right phrase, '. . . genetically modifieds.'

Phoebe nodded. 'My librarian friend told me this story. Kravitz had confided in her and she totally shouldn't have said anything. But I suppose she didn't see the harm and, being a librarian of course, she couldn't resist sharing a little gossip.'

Taking a sip of her drink, Phoebe leant close across the table. 'The thing that really obsessed Dr Kravitz was the connection between certain genes and personality. In particular something he called the moral gene. In order to test his theory he needed a quite different environment for a guinea pig to grow up in. With me so far?'

182

Kai nodded.

'Dr Kravitz dreamt up this experiment to test some of his theories. The government gave him the go-ahead and when we were all still babies, one of his team, his partner in fact, with the help of the SIA, went to live in Downtown under an assumed identity. As a Portobellan. She took a baby boy with her.'

'Took?'

'We guinea pigs don't have parents,' said Phoebe. 'We belong to NebTech. She was going to bring him up as her child, in the Downtown environment. So they would have someone to compare to the ones growing up in the laboratory. So they could see how the specially selected genes fared under the much tougher conditions.'

'What happened?'

'Unfortunately, Dr Kravitz's partner died.' Phoebe reached for her drink again. This time she gulped. 'The young boy was left to fend for himself.'

Kai frowned and turned to the window. He could feel himself trembling. It was like the storm wave's sound. A trembling, groaning rumble, deep down inside.

Outside it was raining hard. He wanted to be out there. In the rain. 'Do you . . .' His throat dried. He swallowed some drink. 'Do you . . . know the woman's name?'

Phoebe bit her lip. She nodded and, reaching across the table, took his hand. 'Ana.'

Kai covered his mouth. It was the name Mushirah had told him. He looked away. *Hold it back*. Beyond the rain-spattered window, white lightning danced like a skeleton in the sky. Like a door slamming, the thunderclap exploded across the harbour.

36

Storm Brewing

Kai felt the vibrations as another wave struck the far side of the high wall. The spray, shooting over the parapet, had a violet glow in the dark. It seemed to hang in the air for a moment before it slapped down hard on the path, foamed over the edge and returned to the sea. There were no keen anglers waiting, rods poised, for a bite tonight.

Where was Mendel? He had said the lighthouse. But with the waves growing bigger and angrier by the minute, the path along the harbour wall was already extremely dangerous. Soon it might be impassable.

Hurrying along the last stretch, Kai peered into the darkness. Not a sign of anyone. Had Mendel been swept into the sea? Had he intended for *him* to be swept away – was that why he'd arranged to meet him at this place? That didn't make sense, Mendel wanted Phoebe. Desperately.

Beyond the lighthouse the waves looked massive. Terrifying. The lighthouse itself provided some protection, but waiting at this spot for more than a few minutes would have been impossible without it. Wave after wave crashed against the wall, every third or fourth sending more spray cascading over.

He heard the throb of powerful engines first, then a dark shape became visible, crashing from crest to crest as the craft slowed, turned and coasted into the harbour. One of the Nebulese Navy's small, fast patrol ships. The engines changed pitch – reverse thrust. In bright yellow water-proofs, a marine jumped, a rope was flung and, with a little difficulty, the boat was moored.

As Kai scurried out from the shadows of the lighthouse, the marine gave a hasty salute and gestured towards the boat. The ship showed no lights on deck but there were figures manning the small cannon. The guns followed Kai as he descended the ladder set into the harbour wall. The ship rose up then fell away again beneath him, a distance several times his height. Two yellow-clad marines beckoned to him from the deck. As the ship lifted once more, he leapt.

Below decks Kai was escorted along a short corridor to a cabin. The marine knocked, saluted and held the door open for Kai.

'You made it!' Mendel rose as Kai entered. 'Well done.' He shook his hand warmly, thanked and dismissed the marine. 'There are towels if you need them.' He gestured. 'Please, help yourself.'

'There's not a lot of point.' Kai was wet beyond what a towel could dry. The seaspray had soaked through to his skin. It felt good. 'I'll be going back out before long.'

Mendel indicated an armchair. 'Make yourself com-fortable.'

'I'll stand.'

'Suit yourself.' Mendel studied his face, trying to interpret the mood.

Kai could have told him. *Raging*.

'So . . . what happened to the girl? You were going to bring her. Did she have an accident too?'

185

'No,' said Kai. 'She's still alive.'

'Fine,' said Mendel. 'You have her somewhere?'

Kai nodded.

'Good work.' Relief flickered across Mendel's face. 'Excellent. Can we get hold of her quickly?'

Kai shook his head.

The relief seeped away. Mendel glanced at his watch. 'The deadline was supposed to be midnight.'

Kai shrugged.

Mendel frowned. 'I don't understand.'

'Phoebe's not coming back.'

'*What?*'

Kai watched Mendel struggle for composure. Beneath the cool exterior he was starting to sweat.

'Is this some kind of trust problem? If you're concerned we'll not keep our side of the bargain, I could take you to Nebula right now.'

'She's not coming back.'

Mendel shook his head. 'You're not being very helpful here. What are you saying – you have the girl but you're not going to hand her over?'

'That's right.'

Mendel laughed uneasily. 'What about the Nebulese citizenship? I thought you wanted that?'

'It's not yours to give,' said Kai.

'What? What do you mean?' said Mendel. 'I spoke to the president personally.'

Kai shrugged. 'Not even the president can grant me something that is already mine.'

Mendel's thin face seemed to quiver. He cocked his head. 'Already yours?'

'I was born in Nebula,' said Kai. 'That makes me Nebulese.' He watched Mendel feign he had no idea what this was about. But of course he did. Kai clenched his fist. 'Please don't insult me by pretending ignorance.'

Anger and resentment clamoured to be let loose. Kai took a deep breath, narrowed his eyes. *Control.* 'You know everything about every Nebulese citizen. You know exactly who I am. It was your organization that helped put me in Portobello in the first place.'

Colour drained from Mendel's face. He stared, lost for words.

'I don't know the full story yet,' said Kai, 'but Dr Kravitz's special project didn't quite go according to plan.' He could see the recognition in Mendel's face. 'Then one day there's a problem with two runaways. Conveniently for you, one of your genetically modified guinea pigs is already in place. And even better, working in the right trade.'

'That's not exactly . . .'

'Don't!' Kai glared. 'Don't try to bullshit me! I *know*.'

'Please.' Mendel's face had a look of desperation. 'Remember what's at stake. This is about much more than you . . . and the girl.'

'Not for me it isn't.'

'Portobello's future hangs in the balance.'

'Having persuaded me to track down two fellow victims of NebTech, one of whom is now dead, you're asking me to hand over the other to be your prisoner? And what about me? Do I give myself up too? Am I free to do what I want?'

'We can come to a deal. Nebula *has* to have you and the girl back. You're in excellent positions to negotiate. Do it together if you wish. The pair of you could do very well for yourselves.'

Kai stared directly into Mendel's eyes. 'Now that I know

I'm Nebulese, I'm ashamed.' He shook his head. 'You are my people. My people did this to me. Did what's been done to Phoenix, Phoebe and the others at NebTech's laboratory. It is my people who attack Portobello with Black Widow gunships.'

For once Mendel had no reply.

'I've never felt like I belonged in Downtown. If the future of Portobello hangs in the balance, that is not my responsibility.' Kai shook his head. 'I can no more guarantee the city's safety by negotiating with you than I can guarantee my own. Phoebe and I may have something you want but how could we ever trust you?' He took a step towards Mendel. 'I'm afraid you're wrong. The future of Portobello is not in my hands. It's in yours. It is *your* responsibility.'

Kai turned and headed for the door. 'I have always trusted my instinct. My gut feeling about you has always been good. For Portobello's sake, I hope you do the right thing.'

37

Headstrong and Stubborn

From the small covered porch of the lifeguard's cabin, Kai gazed out at the grey-green ocean. With its subtle lulling rhythms, somehow it could soothe the most troubled mind.

The wind had dropped. The rain had slowed to a delicate drizzle. The world appeared tranquil. Yet twice in the night he had heard the discordant groans of the coming storm wave. 'Seismic' sounds, Phoebe had called them. The sound of rock strata shifting and grinding against one another, deep below the ocean. That made sense.

He had recounted the tale about the storm wave of his childhood, explaining the connection to those noises. The story had alarmed her. She hadn't known about the wave or the devastation it had caused in Downtown. But she had read about underwater earthquakes and landslides, and the pattern of build-up he had described chimed with her understanding of how storm waves were generated. The seismic activity could cause enormous waves that travelled across whole oceans.

Incredibly, when he had told her about his plan to escape on the wave, instead of laughing she had listened in interested silence. And when he'd finished, she had told him she wanted to go with him. She wanted to go *with him*! She seemed to view escape as some kind of moral duty. As far as she was concerned, death was a risk worth taking to keep Nebula from controlling the two of them and their special genes.

That thought had deeply gratified him. After everything she'd told him about who he was, he so wanted to get back at Nebula. In his initial maelstrom of rage he had even thought he might join the freedom fighters. But now there was a better way of exacting revenge. If he and Phoebe could escape, they took with them the one thing Nebula most treasured. Something Nebula was desperate not to share with the world.

Phoebe was tough and direct. He liked her. They were getting on well. After the unexpected twists of the last few days, it looked as if things at last might settle.

'Morning.' Stretching and yawning, Phoebe shuffled out on to the veranda. Blurry-eyed still, she surveyed the damp but becalmed world. She had forgotten how high off the ground they were.

Kai turned. Smiled. 'How did you sleep?'

'I never knew lifejackets could make such a comfortable mattress!' She squatted beside him. 'Been up all night?'

He shrugged.

She knew he had. Her own sleep had been fitful, her mind too busy for proper slumber. She had seen him, perched by the window, keeping watch. 'I've been thinking . . .'

'Change of heart?'

She shook her head. 'No.'

'Then what?'

'There's something else. Something I think we've overlooked.' She knew he wasn't going to like this.

He cocked his head, waiting.

Deep breath. 'What about Downtown? The people?'

'I don't get you.'

190

'Last time the wave came you said it caused terrible destruction. Lots of people lost their lives.'

Kai looked away. 'People die in Downtown every day.'

'Yes, but if you're so sure another wave's coming . . .'

'Next two or three days. Guaranteed.'

She leant towards him. 'Don't you think we ought to warn them?'

He laughed.

She didn't see what was so funny. 'What?'

'You and me? Warn the people of Downtown about the storm wave?'

'Yes!'

'How are we going to do that, then? Stand up on a street corner and proclaim it, like poor old Mushirah, the blind woman?'

'We could try.'

'No one listened to her. Who's going to listen to us?'

'We could tell them who we are. Tell them how we know.'

'Oh yeah, that'll go down well! "We're genetic freaks from Nebula. We can hear the earth shifting. And we think you should know a giant storm wave is on the way." I can see it now. They'd stone us to death!'

She wanted to slap him. OK. So she hadn't thought this through clearly. But she hadn't had time. 'Well, what do you suggest?'

'We go to the headland. Get ready. Wait for the wave.'

'That's it?' He was deliberately refusing to see her point, she knew. 'What about all those people drowning?'

He groaned. 'Look. If there was a simple, practical way to warn people without putting ourselves in mortal danger, I'd consider it. Maybe. But there isn't.'

'You've barely given it a moment's thought!' Arrogant,

191

selfish know-all. 'If you won't help me, I'll do it on my own!' Turning, she stormed down the steps, and stomped off up the beach.

This was madness. Why was he doing this? What had he been thinking – to have shared his plans with this almost total stranger? Only twenty-four hours ago he had been hunting her down as a fugitive. Now, here he was, chasing after her through the streets of Portobello as a . . . what? A friend?

He was losing his judgement.

At least for the time being she had abandoned grabbing people and yelling at them that the giant wave was coming. Too many had laughed at her or pushed her away.

Why was he still following her? Why not just let her do whatever it was she felt she had to do? He could turn round now. Get down to the headland and wait for that wave. If she wanted to join him, fine. If not, that was her problem.

He liked her. More than that. She was like him. She was the only person in the world he had met like him. She had told him there were others, but they were locked away somewhere in a laboratory complex. He didn't know them. Never would. But Phoebe was different. She was here. She mattered.

He had the *XK7*. He had removed and disposed of the transmitter device last night, but hopefully the gun still worked. He could try threatening her, make her give up her foolishness and come with him. But he knew that wouldn't work. She was too headstrong and stubborn. She would call his bluff. She was like him.

She was also tired and disillusioned. She had been trying but getting nowhere for more than two hours now. All he had to do was wait. Pretty soon she would give up.

*

Was she being a fool? She didn't think so. OK, maybe stopping people in the street and telling them to flee for their lives wasn't proving so effective, but how else could she warn them? What she was trying to do was right. She knew it was.

She stopped and turned round. He was there, twenty paces behind her. Wet and bedraggled, like her, with his hood up. Still following her.

'You haven't gone to the headland.'

Kai shook his head as he approached. 'There's time yet.'

'Did you hear that last one?'

Kai nodded. 'Longest yet. The episodes are bunching up now. It's coming without a doubt. I reckon two or three more and it'll be on its way.'

'Look, you think I'm wasting my time. And I agree.'

He frowned at first, wary of a trap. Then smiled.

Seeing the smugness, she so wanted to slap him. 'I'm getting nowhere. It's wet. No one wants to stop and listen. And anyway, it would take me forever to warn enough people.'

That told-you-so smirk. 'So?'

'I've got a proposal.'

'Go on, then.'

'One last try at warning, then I'll come with you to the headland. And we can wait for the wave.'

He waited.

'I'll need your help.' Just the smallest of pouts. 'Any chance?'

'That depends. What's the plan?'

'I'm going to talk to the Portobellan government.'

'What!?' Kai's face clouded. 'You're *insane*!'

*

What was he doing here? It was stark staring lunacy. And he had told her so, over and over.

He had survived all these years in Downtown. When the opportunity knocked, he had devised a masterful escape plan. He had trained for it. He had made the mistake of being sidetracked on one last job, worked for the SIA, been shot, come close to falling into Medusa, and had his whole universe turned upside down. But still he had won through and taken things in hand. He could leave now. Everything was set up to put the escape plan into action.

But no.

She had tricked him – bewitched him, persuaded him, whatever – somehow she had got him this far. He was doing it. For her.

The government of Portobello. It wasn't going to be what she expected. The council and their leader were little better than gangsters and used the city's militia force as their own private army. People complained, but the council got re-elected by a landslide every time because no one dared stand against them. Portobello was a rough, tough city to govern and the council did the job.

'That's the place.' Kai nodded towards the bullet-scarred building across the road. Government House. Where the council met to discuss important matters.

Disappointment fell like a veil across Phoebe's face.

'Keep walking. Don't stare.' He nudged her forwards. 'We're trying not to draw attention to ourselves, remember?'

'But it looks like a fortress,' she groaned. 'There are guards all over the front steps. The street's crawling with militia.'

'What did you expect? Just knock at the door and wander in?'

Phoebe scowled. 'The outside world is still new to me, remember.'

Kai led her across the road towards a street down the side of Government House. If they followed it to the end it would bring them back round towards the piazza. 'Do you see now,' he said, 'why I had such doubts? Why don't we head back to Downtown and get ourselves ready to leave?'

Phoebe stopped in her tracks. 'I haven't come all this way just to give up.'

He'd been afraid she'd say that.

'I was ingenious and adept enough to escape from NebTech's laboratory complex. You've . . .' She trailed off. 'I don't actually know what you've done or do, apart from hunting down fugitives.'

Now probably wasn't a good time to explain.

'But I'm sure you're capable of a little stealth and ingenuity too.' She angled her gaze up at the side of the building. 'There must be other ways in.'

Phoebe felt sick. Badly. Like she might vomit any second. The only thing stopping her was pride. Kai had puked yesterday. To hold the moral high ground she had to prove herself tougher than him. Determined that she would, she covered her mouth and nose with her hand.

She had imagined them finding their way into the building by some devious rooftop route, then down through a skylight or some such. But that way, Kai had insisted, would be too heavily guarded because the main source of threat was always helicopter gunships. He'd been up there and seen it with his own eyes. So he said.

So here they were, up to their ankles in – she couldn't bear to think about it . . . trudging along a sewerage pipe beneath the city. Still, they were doing it, that was the main thing.

Ahead, the slooshing sound of Kai's footsteps halted. 'There's a steel grating blocking our path.' His face loomed out of the darkness in front of her. 'This must be where the building starts.'

'Will we have to turn back?'

'Depends on the gaps. Let's see.'

Apart from the flame of Kai's lighter, it was total blackness. The flame died. She couldn't see what he was doing but she supposed he must be trying to feel if there was a way to squeeze between the bars.

'We're in luck!' Kai struck another flame. 'This grate was built to keep out chunky Nebulese marines. There's a gap I'm pretty sure we could get through.'

'Great.'

'I'm not sure you'll think so when I tell you where it is.'

'Oh?' She didn't like his tone – a note of gloat again. 'Where, then?'

'Between the bottom bar of the grate and the floor of the pipe.'

In the dark, it took her a moment to picture what he meant. Then she realized. 'You mean we have to get down in the . . .'

' 'Fraid so,' said Kai. 'In the shit.' He struck the lighter, illuminating his face. 'If you're up for that then . . .' He grinned and gestured towards the grating. 'After you.'

38

Abomination

To have got this far during daylight hours was good going. They'd been fortunate, he had to admit. Like everything in Portobello, the security at Government House was inept and ill thought out. Using the sewerage system had been an inspired last-minute, last-resort improvisation. He hadn't expected it to provide access to this particular building.

They had finally scrambled up a short, narrow shaft and come out in the kitchen courtyard. Phoebe hadn't spoken for some time. He could tell she was furious. She stank and was sulking. That didn't make the task ahead any easier.

'OK.' He had to get close to whisper. Phoebe scowled at his reticence. 'The debating chamber is up on the second level. There's a public gallery on the third. Take your pick.'

Phoebe continued to scowl. She said nothing.

'Hey, you're not still mad at me about the grate?'

'The grate?' Her jaw was clenched. 'Why would I be?'

He shrugged. 'Because of its coming loose? I mean after you had got down in all that . . .' stifling a snigger he lowered his eyes. 'I hope you don't think that was deliberate?' She did. He could see it in her eyes. But he hadn't known. He should have maybe tried giving the grate a yank, before she got herself all messy, but it hadn't occurred to him. The bars had looked so solid. It was the concrete that had crumbled and given way. So she was soiled and he wasn't. 'You still want to go ahead?'

'Yes.'

Having briefly explained the plan, he led the way. The door from yard to kitchen had been left ajar by the smokers whose cigarette butts littered the ground. Slipping indoors, he and Phoebe crept low behind a row of big ovens. The kitchen's noise and bustle were good for going unnoticed. And with a bit of luck, the cooking aromas might mask Phoebe's special smell as they passed through. A short dash across an aisle then an easy scurry behind the worktops.

With a glance to check for watching eyes, Kai darted for cover down the side of a large refrigerator. A small door, waist height on the wall, caught his attention. Sliding it open, he peered inside. Perfect! He beckoned to Phoebe.

Crouching low, she hurried over.

'Climb in,' he hissed.

'What? In there? What is it?'

'A dumb waiter,' he whispered, pushing her towards it. 'A small elevator. It carries food between floors.' There wasn't time to explain. Bundling her inside and shoving her towards the back, he hopped in next to her and slapped the button on the wall.

Where would they end up?

Phoebe pressed herself flat against the door frame. So this was it. Unbelievably, Kai had got them here, to a corridor running along the side of the debating chamber. Luckily, the state dining room had been unstaffed when the dumb waiter had whirred to a halt on the second floor. But she had to admit – to herself at any rate – she had developed a sneaking respect for Kai's skill and judgment in bringing them this far.

He was cleverly cautious. And yet took outrageous risks. So far they had all paid off. As they had exited the dining room into a silent corridor, he'd suddenly dragged her into the women's toilet and told her to strip. She had frozen for a moment, thinking he had some new humiliation planned. But he was just being smart. She was already soaked. A few minutes washing her clothes might get rid of the stench, he had suggested. As she still planned on addressing the council, the less she stank the better.

And of course, annoyingly, he'd been right.

She sniffed. Did she still stink? All she could smell was the soap. The worst of it had gone, that was the main thing. As she hurried towards Kai, who was beckoning from the far end of the corridor, she couldn't help smirking to herself. Her boots, now waterlogged, squeaked when she walked.

Kai pulled her into a stairwell. 'What's funny?' He scowled.

She stifled a snort. 'I'm sorry. My boots are squeaking . . . and I think my heart is about to explode, it's racing so fast. My nerves are jangled.'

He gripped her by the shoulders. She could feel herself shaking. Green eyes, like hers. 'Why don't we just give up? Go back now.'

'No.'

'You're still determined?'

She nodded. She was terrified. But she knew she had to do it. She had to try.

'There are guards round the front. That means no way are we getting in on this floor. I saw PFF fighters hanging around too. It must be some kind of special meeting.'

'That would explain the heavy security?'

Kai nodded. 'The building must be closed to ordinary

citizens.' His eyes pointed up the stairs. 'The public gallery looks like our only chance.'

'OK.' She began to climb.

'I'm not sure what you're expecting, or if you've got anything planned . . .'

Of course she hadn't. When had she had a moment to *plan*? Other than that she was going to walk in there and open her mouth. 'I'm going to play it by ear.'

'That's kind of what I assumed.' As Kai hurried ahead, he pulled out his gun.

The public gallery was completely empty. No guards at either entrance too. All well and good. Moving silently and bent low behind the seats, Kai made his way down to the front of the balcony, beckoning to Phoebe to follow.

Voices raised in anger rose up from the debating chamber below. It sounded as if everyone was shouting at once. Council members and uniformed freedom fighters remonstrated with one another, gesticulating and shaking their fists. Kai was relieved to see no one appeared to be carrying weapons. A wise precaution, perhaps, given the level of anger in the air.

Phoebe crouched beside him, her face ashen, her pupils wildly dilated.

He smiled to reassure her. 'Ready for this?'

She managed a smile. 'No!'

'I'm going to be watching our backs. When I say it's time to run, we go. No questions. Deal?'

She nodded. 'Of course.' Reaching for his hand, she lowered her eyes. 'I'm sorry for dragging you into this.' Her voice shook.

'Don't be.' He grinned. 'I came of my own accord. Danger is my middle name!'

Her smile trembled. 'Thanks.'

A thick rope had been tied round a front row seat. Kai had noticed it there when he first entered the gallery. The rope ran taut over the balcony and down into the debating chamber below. Now, as he and Phoebe listened to the disorderly shouting, trying to grasp the tenor of the argument, he noticed it again. And a terrible uneasy feeling crept over him.

'This behaviour,' bellowed a faceless voice, 'is indefensible!'

'We acted from frustration and desperation.'

'You have shown total disrespect!'

'It is an abomination!'

Indicating for Phoebe to stay put, Kai made his way past the rope, towards the far side of the balcony. He had to see down into the chamber. He had to find out. What was on the end of that rope?

'You are no better than a pack of wild animals!'

'And you are fat lazy imbeciles who need a good kick up the . . .'

'How dare you desecrate this place, the grand seat of all Portobellan government and law?'

'How dare you spew such empty hypocritical hyperbole?'

'We invited you to debate our current crisis. And you have brought shame and disrepute on the council.'

'This is anarchy!'

Reaching the furthest corner of the balcony, Kai slowly straightened up and peered over the edge.

There, dangling on the end of the rope, his worst fears were confirmed. A bloated body. The head over to one side, slumped against the chest. The noose tight round the neck. Though the face was obscured, Kai didn't need a glimpse to recognize the victim. *Paps.*

'If we'd waited for you and your corrupt idiot militia to act, nothing would ever have been done!' A furious, goatee-bearded, PFF fighter pointed at the swinging corpse and glared at an older man across the debating floor. 'We executed a traitor. A collaborator. Nothing more.'

Kai recognized the older man with greying hair. He had seen him at rallies and on posters across the town. Jordy Lodestone, leader of the council. Portobello's Eminent Member. Jordy stepped forwards and waited for the heckling to cease. 'What has happened in this chamber today is a terrible travesty. No word of it must leave the building.'

The grave silence which seemed to fall upon the assembled council members and freedom fighters was suddenly broken by a faint coughing sound.

Kai glanced across to where Phoebe had been hiding. Oh no! She was up on her feet, staring down into the debating chamber.

'Excuse me . . .'

As one, the gathered council members and freedom fighters looked up and glanced around.

'I realize this is a very awkward time . . .' Phoebe coughed to clear her throat. 'But what I have to say cannot wait.' Her voice was quivering. 'If you would please just listen for one minute, the enormous importance of what I have to tell you will become clear.'

The men and women below stared in stunned amazement, fury, outrage.

'In the next twelve to thirty-six hours an enormous tidal wave will strike these shores. There's every reason to believe this one will have similar devastating consequences to the one of a decade ago.'

Kai had kept down low, out of sight. But from his

position he could see some council members and PFF fighters were already shaking themselves from the spell.

'If you act swiftly,' Phoebe's voice was gaining confidence, 'you will still have time to warn your people. In particular the residents of Downtown, who, being on the lowest slopes, must be in the most danger. You have it within your power to avert a major human catastrophe. Something I'm sure you all want to do . . .' She trailed off.

Kai saw a council member hurrying towards the exit, a freedom fighter close behind him. Others were turning to one another, muttering and gesticulating. Kai beckoned to Phoebe. But she was in a trance, too intent on her audience to notice.

'Who the hell are you?' boomed a voice.

'Please do this!' Phoebe's voice croaked with desperation. 'You could save hundreds, probably thousands of lives!'

Kai whistled, loud and shrill. As everyone turned to look, he made his way round the balcony towards Phoebe. 'If you want your little scandal to stay secret,' he yelled, pointing down at Paps's swinging corpse, 'I suggest you do something worthwhile for a change. Do as my friend asks!'

Phoebe was staring at him.

'Come on.' He smiled. 'Time to go!'

39

Special Dumplings

'The look on that chef's face!' Phoebe laughed.

Jumping to his feet, Kai did an impression. 'I thought he was going to skewer you on the end of his kebab sticks!'

'I don't think the kitchen staff knew what had hit them!'

Pursued by security guards, they had fled to the state dining room and exited the way they had arrived – via the dumb waiter. But on the ground floor there had been a welcoming party. Deafened by the shrill alarms, the two of them had been forced to run the gauntlet of the kitchen, dodging this way and that as staff struggled desperately to stop them.

'But we made it,' said Kai. 'That's the thing. Now it's all down to Jordy Lodestone and his cronies.'

Back in the safety of the lifeguards' cabin it was easy to laugh. They were sitting on lifejackets, sipping hot black tea which he had conjured on the stove in the back.

Phoebe sighed; her body seemed to deflate. She looked exhausted. Kai reached over and put an arm round her shoulders. 'You did what you set out to do. It was very courageous. You couldn't have done more.'

Phoebe gave a feeble nod. 'Do you think they'll take any notice?'

Kai shrugged. He doubted it. 'I'm not a good person to ask.'

'No. I suppose not.' Phoebe looked into his face. 'What if the wave doesn't come?'

'It will.' It wasn't time yet but they needed to be getting ready. 'Three bouts of noise in twenty-four hours. The same pattern I remember from all those years ago. Maybe one or two more episodes. The final one will be massive. Louder and much scarier than the others. And going on for longer.' He tapped his skull. 'I'll never forget it.'

'After we hear that, the wave will be on its way?'

He nodded. 'Arriving within the hour. But we've still got a little time yet.'

'Good!' Phoebe rubbed her stomach and groaned. 'I need to eat.'

'Definitely.' Kai was starving. He felt drained too. No wonder. When had he last eaten? He couldn't remember. And he'd vomited since. Getting to his feet, he held out his hand to Phoebe. 'It's time you tried the best food in Portobello.'

The piazza was empty again. Rain and seaspray were once more being whipped up by gusting gale-force winds. The few intrepid Downtowners out and about scurried fast, hugging walls for shelter.

Kai and Phoebe, hooded and booted, ran splashing towards the Green Star Noodle Bar. From the open doorway Clod waved and beckoned. They charged past him up the steps and collapsed, soaking wet, breathless and laughing.

Clod closed the door behind them. 'Welcome!' His eyes flitted from Kai to Phoebe and back again. He frowned, puzzled. 'I was worried about you.'

'Worried?' Kai shook himself like a wet dog. 'About *me*!?' He could see Clod was baffled by Phoebe's presence;

205

so much had happened since finding her on the boat. 'When have you ever known anything bad befall me?'

Clod snorted. 'Here! Dry yourselves.' He tossed serviettes to each of them. 'I'll get you some towels.'

'This will do fine,' said Kai. 'I've been wet through so many times I'm getting used to it now.'

Phoebe nodded. 'Me too.'

Clod glanced at Kai. 'I was beginning to wonder if we'd ever see you again.'

'I told you I'd drop by.'

Clod nodded. 'I thought you might have already moved to Nebula.'

'Changed my mind,' said Kai.

Clod glanced towards Phoebe. 'Turning soft?'

Kai lunged, wide-eyed and aggressive, making Clod jump with fright. 'No,' said Kai, laughing. 'Not soft. I just couldn't trust the Nebs. Much as I wanted to.'

'You love Downtown too much,' chuckled Clod. 'That's your problem. You couldn't bring yourself to leave.'

'How little you know me!' Kai nodded towards Phoebe. 'Trouble is, now I'm not dealing with the Nebs, I'm stuck with *her*.' Phoebe's eyes narrowed, her nostrils flared. Kai winked.

Clod turned to Phoebe. 'What do you make of our city?'

She scowled. 'I think it's a terrible, barbaric place. Full of wretched, uncivilized people.'

Kai chuckled. 'She loves it really.'

'Well . . .' Clod rubbed his hands together. 'I don't know what the two of you've been up to, but you both look starved.' He gestured to a large table in the corner. 'Why don't you stay and eat something?'

Kai looked around. The place was practically deserted.

'Don't worry,' said Clod. 'Paps still isn't back.'

206

'No?' Kai shuddered. Should he tell Clod? He glanced at Phoebe, drying her hair. Had she seen the swinging body? She wouldn't have known who it was, of course. He handed the serviette back to Clod. 'How you coping?'

'This weather's not good for business,' said Clod. 'Most of our trade's from the market.' He nodded towards the piazza. 'On days like this, everyone stays at home.' He shrugged. 'We're doing OK.'

'That wasn't what I meant.'

Clod moved a little closer. 'To be honest,' he said, 'it's been nice without Paps around. I'm more relaxed. So are the staff. I can run this place without him, no problem.'

'You're not worried?'

Clod shrugged. 'Who knows where he's got to? Plenty of buildings were turned to rubble in the last Neb raid.'

'He could be dead and buried?'

Clod nodded. 'If Paps didn't come back for some reason . . .' Glancing around nervously, he lowered his voice, 'I w-w-wouldn't miss him.'

Kai patted Clod's cheek and smiled. Clod looked taller now, less cowed. Paps had treated him like a dog. 'Never thought you'd find the courage to say it. And d'you know what,' said Kai, 'you didn't stutter once, till just now.'

Clod smiled back, embarrassed. He glanced at Phoebe. 'Sit down and I'll bring some food.' He slapped Kai's stomach. 'You need firebeans in your belly!'

It was still day, but it was dark outside. Shutters flapped and banged against their catches, windows shuddered in their frames, rain and seawater rattled against the panes. Driving it all, the wind ripped round the Green Star Noodle Bar without let-up, whistling against the eaves.

The restaurant had very few customers. Kai and Phoebe

207

sat at a candlelit table. Clod had brought over their food and now sat with them to eat. Neither Kai nor Phoebe had eaten in a long time; they were both eating fast and furious.

'This is excellent,' said Kai. 'Better than ever.'

Phoebe nodded. 'Delicious! In Nebula we eat with knife and fork, but I prefer it like this, with fingers.'

The table was crowded with food: fried fish, and grilled meats, sauces and dips, savoury pastries, dumplings and small pies, bowls of noodles, a selection of vegetables and several different kinds of bread. There were plenty of dishes Kai did not recognize and had to test by taste.

'Mmm! So much food!' said Kai between mouthfuls. 'Clod's father always made him bring me just the house special,' he said. 'Whenever I came to do work for him.'

'With extra firebeans,' said Clod.

Kai nodded. 'Always with extra firebeans.'

'Um!' Phoebe's hand shot to her mouth. 'Hot!' She fanned her mouth with her fingers. 'Firebeans . . . good!'

Clod and Kai exchanged smiles.

'But these,' said Kai, holding up a dumpling between his finger and thumb, 'these are the best thing I have ever eaten!'

'My new creation,' said Clod. 'Glad you like them. I'm thinking they should become part of the house special from now on.'

'What's in them?' said Phoebe, grabbing one and popping it into her mouth.

'A real Downtown delicacy,' said Clod.

Nudging his foot under the table, Kai winked. 'Crispy glazed cockroach!'

'*Phleeeaugh!*' Phoebe coughed, her eyes bulged as if she were about to choke, then her lips burst apart and she sprayed the contents of her mouth across the table. '*Eeaugh!* Yuk! Yuk-yuk-yuk!'

Kai and Clod fell about laughing.

'You'll have to excuse my lady friend,' said Kai. 'She's from Nebula. They have quite different ideas about grace and etiquette.'

Phoebe glared.

'Downtown humour,' Kai smiled. Grabbing another dumpling, he bit it in half. 'They're not really cockroach. Here . . .' He offered Phoebe the other portion. 'It's king prawn. Go on!'

'No way!' Shaking her head, she pushed it from her. She shivered, as a gust of wind howled round the building. Then she froze.

Kai heard it, the same moment he saw Phoebe's expression change. It was happening again. Mother Earth was groaning, as she prepared to give birth.

Clod stared, transfixed by Phoebe's face.

As Clod turned to look at him, Kai realized his own expression must be a similar picture of terror. It was impossible to hear the noise and not feel fear. Instinctively he had covered his ears with his hands, though he knew it could not block out the sound. 'It's the storm wave,' he said. 'I can hear it grumbling again.'

Clod's eyes darted from Kai to Phoebe, then back again. He frowned, puzzled. 'She hears it too!'

The worst of the noise was dissipating. Kai nodded. 'Phoebe's like me.'

Clod's frown deepened.

'Or, maybe it makes more sense to say that I'm like her.'

'How d'you mean?' Clod's mouth dropped. 'Oh my God! She's a . . . you mean you're . . .'

Kai nodded.

Clod gawped in dumbstruck silence.

'Pretty incredible, huh?' Kai sighed.

Clod grunted.

'I found it difficult to take in at first too – but it all fits. It's a long story.'

'Must be.' Clod looked dazed. 'So, er, this storm wave business . . . it's real?'

Kai and Phoebe nodded as one.

'You still plan to try and use it to escape?'

'The big trip.' Kai nodded. 'And now I have someone to travel with.' He smiled at Phoebe. 'We should make our preparations.'

Phoebe nodded. 'And get down to that headland.'

'You're both crazy,' said Clod. 'No one else would venture out in this weather, let alone go clambering around down there.' He shook his head. 'Let alone try and do what you're planning to do.'

'The truth is,' said Kai, 'the headland is probably the safest place to be. It's high. If this storm wave is anything like the last one, Downtown is going to take a pounding.'

'Maybe I should come with you, then?' Clod grinned. 'To the headland, I mean.'

'That's what I was going to suggest,' said Kai. 'Pack a few things. I can show you places to shelter. You'll be safe there when the wave hits.' He got to his feet. 'It's time we got going. Meet us in an hour, on Gorgon's Rest.'

40

Storm Wave

Clod felt proud. He had set off as soon as he'd packed. Then he'd climbed all the way to Gorgon's Rest without pause. And under such arduous conditions!

Sitting on his very full backpack, he tried in vain to shelter beneath an oilskin. He'd carried it expressly for that purpose but the wind was too strong and whichever way he attempted to arrange things, after only a few seconds the oilskin was flapping wildly around his ears again. Time to give up. Rain had soaked through everything during the course of his slow climb, anyway.

Despite the water dripping from his eyebrows and nose, he felt a deep sense of satisfaction as he sat and watched the two figures approaching up the slope.

A few minutes later Kai and Phoebe trudged to a stop in front of him and flopped, panting, to the ground. He grinned. 'What took you so long?'

Phoebe groaned. 'We had stuff to collect. And then, as we set off, the militia started driving around warning people to flee to higher ground in the north of the city. It got a bit chaotic.'

'Sounds like your storm wave's official.'

Kai and Phoebe grinned.

'We might have had something to do with that,' said Kai. He eyed Clod's fat backpack. 'Travelling light, I see!'

Clod shrugged. 'Thought the three of us might be up here for a while.'

Kai shook his head. 'The massive seismic rumble I'd been expecting came as we were climbing. The wave is on its way.'

'It was terrifying,' said Phoebe. 'Like an enormous explosion deep inside the planet.'

'We haven't got long.' Lifting a thick coil of rope he had slung over his shoulder, Kai unstrapped a package from his back and held it out to Clod. 'For you.'

Clod stared. 'What is it?'

'A lifejacket. Just in case. I borrowed it from the lifeguards' cabin. Keep it on till the storm wave has gone.'

With Kai helping him, Clod obeyed.

'Hey!' yelled Phoebe. 'D'you hear that?'

Clod cocked his head. 'All I can hear is the wind,' he yelled.

'No,' said Phoebe. 'It's something else. It didn't sound like the seismic noises. Maybe it's the wave . . .'

Kai nodded. 'Whatever it is, I hear it too. We should get down to the cliff's edge straight away.' He checked Clod's lifejacket was securely tied. 'Right! Best leave your other stuff here.'

Kai led the way, past the crumbling stone plinth and down towards the path to the viewing platform. He glanced at Phoebe. Her face was set. Was she remembering the drama that had been played out here?

Medusa's tails of spume soared high into the air. Her writhing, thrashing serpents came into view. She seemed now to gyrate more furiously than ever, as though she sensed somehow what was coming. Kai stared into the dark, swirling vortex. Would his plan work? Could

Medusa be overwhelmed by the storm wave long enough for them to make their escape?

'*Look!*' Clod was pointing out to sea, his eyes wide in shock.

Kai stared. Below the horizon, there was another line. It trembled.

'Oh my God!' Phoebe's jaw dropped.

Kai shivered. 'You beauty!' The moment he'd been waiting for, preparing for all this time, *all his life*, was here. The Wave!

Clod shook his head. 'I never actually b-b-believed . . .'

'I know.' Kai smiled. 'But it's true.'

Now rain and spray were blowing in off the sea at full pelt. Phoebe had already begun removing her outer garments. Shaking himself from his trance, Kai followed suit. Clod turned away from them both, embarrassed.

Phoebe had stripped to a bikini. Tied to each ankle, she wore a knife in a leather sheath. A couple of small leather pouches were tightly strapped at her waist. Nothing else.

Above his swimming briefs Kai also had a belt and leather pouches strapped to his waist. A holster on his hip, strapped at the thigh, carried the *kombatordnantz XK7*.

'That's *it?*' said Clod. 'That's all you're taking with you!?'

Kai nodded. 'To bodysurf we need to be as light and streamlined as possible. And when the wave runs out of energy or drops us, we could have a long way to swim. The less we carry, the better our chances.'

The trembling line drew closer. And as it did so it began to take form. Slowly but surely a wave shape rose up from the ocean.

Kai's eyes flitted across the headland. He needed something to gauge the wave's height against. *Dolphins' Point*. How high would it be when it hit the cliffs he dived from? Any higher and the three of them would be swept away.

From nothing, the wave rose as it advanced. It seemed to be rushing forwards, eager now it was close to meet the land. And towering up, up, up . . .

Kai felt his heart skip a beat. The cliffs below Dolphins' Point had simply vanished, swallowed by the oncoming wall of water.

A grimace of horror spread across Clod's face.

Phoebe looked terrified too. 'It's *massive* . . .' She turned to Kai. 'Isn't it too big?'

He nodded. Grabbing Clod's arm he started to run, dragging him back up towards the stone plinth. 'Come on!' he yelled to Phoebe. 'Bring the rope!'

She caught up with them as they reached the plinth.

Kai snatched the rope. 'Sit! Backs against the stone!'

Clod and Phoebe obeyed, one either side.

Giving Phoebe one end of the rope, Kai dropped between the two of them, passed the rope in front of him and on to Clod. 'Pass it round to Phoebe! *Hurry!*'

Phoebe cottoned on straight away; taking the rope in front of her, she passed it in the same direction, back round to Kai. A complete circle. Kai passed it to Clod again.

The wave was rolling closer, rising along the ridge. A giant wall of water, stretching into the distance as far as the eye could see.

'Breathe in!' yelled Kai. Yanking the rope tight, he knotted it as the dark quivering wall slipped towards the end of the ridge.

The sound was like nothing anyone could have ever heard before. A roaring of such terrible and terrifying loudness it seemed the world must end. Kai watched the wave come, its mighty cresting top spilling over the cliff's edge. One massive wall of water, sucking up everything in its path. Reaching round the plinth, he found Phoebe's hand and Clod's. He squeezed. 'Hold tight! Take a last breath! See you on the other side!'

How long was it? It could only have been a matter of seconds. Kai had tried to count but the force of the water, even though it was just the tiniest tip of the wave that struck them, had been incredible. Thousands of gallons trying to wrench them from their improvised moorings.

The moment the buffeting stopped and his head was clear of the torrent, Kai started unknotting the rope. Phoebe reached round to help.

There was an eerie quiet.

'Clod!' Kai cranked his head round. 'Clod? You OK?'

Coughing and spluttering back to life, Clod nodded.

Kai stared. Beyond Clod, the view of Portobello was obscured by the wave, as it rolled on. He dragged his eyes away. There wasn't time to watch. He had to hurry. The wave was travelling fast. Any second now it would be hitting the shore. Then the rebound wave would be on its way back. That was their ride.

Phoebe was free of the rope.

'Go on!' Kai motioned. 'Get down on the path. Forget about the rope; we won't need to go as far as the platform.'

'What about you?'

'I'll catch up. Go on!'

Scrambling to his feet, Kai helped Clod up. 'Got to go!' he gasped. 'Don't worry. The rebound wave won't reach up here. You're safe, I promise.'

Clod dredged up a brave smile. 'I'm going to m-m-miss you!'

'Live long. And take care!' Kai hugged his befuddled, bedraggled friend. 'Till the next time!' He turned and sprinted for the cliff's edge.

As Kai ran, he felt the ground shake beneath his feet. The wave had struck Downtown!

He reached the cliff path, dizzy with breathlessness. Further down, Phoebe glanced back anxiously, as she picked her way along the treacherous slope.

Kai began the slippery descent. On this side of the headland the wave had further to travel, up the coast and beyond Nebula, before it hit the wall of cliffs that would send it back. But as he hurried he felt the ground shake again and knew the wave had started towards them.

How high would it be this time?

He whistled to Phoebe. 'That's far enough!' Descending towards her, he peered into the distance.

It was coming.

All they had to do was time their moment right – dive into its path and catch its momentum. They had talked it through, over and over. They could do this.

Phoebe was shaking like a leaf. 'I'm *so scared*!'

Taking her hands, Kai squeezed. He was shaking too. 'You'll be fine! You're a natural!'

The roar of the approaching wave was deafening.

Phoebe squeezed back. 'See you at the other end?'

Kai nodded and wrapped his arms around her. 'Be lucky!'

41

Vicious End

Entering the room, Mendel closed the door behind him. Etiquette dictated he advance no further. The president was at the window and had his back to him. He waited.

After a short while, Mendel gave a discreet cough. When the president showed no sign of hearing, showed no response of any kind, he coughed again. 'Excuse me, Mr President, sir?'

'Ah!' The president spun round. 'Mendel! Good.' He gestured. 'Please, have a seat.'

'Thank you, sir.'

'Now . . .' The president seated himself in his throne-like chair behind the enormous desk. 'Things have been a bit hectic, what with Operation Vengeance and then that freak wave hitting the coast. But please don't think *our little problem* has slipped my mind.' He leant forwards, eyes bright and eager. 'What news have you got for me?'

'Well, sir . . .' Mendel took a deep breath. In his head, he'd rehearsed this moment a thousand times. And now it was here. What was he going to say? The president's eyes bored into his, trying to peer behind the mask. *No chance.* 'Our little problem has been solved, sir.' A slight but reassuring smile. 'Mission accomplished.'

'Excellent.' A fleeting scowl betrayed the president's

disappointment. 'Portobello gets a stay of execution.' He gave a low chuckle. 'What's left of it, that is!'

'Yes, sir.'

Opening the platinum cigar box on his desk, the president offered it to Mendel.

'No, thank you, sir.'

Selecting a cigar, the president wafted it under his nose, then held it up to his ear and gently shook it. 'Bring me up to date. The boy, you reckon, died in the whirlpool. What about the girl? Do we have her back?' He snipped the cigar with a pair of scissors. 'Or is she dead too?'

'They are all dead, sir.'

'All?'

'The girl, the boy and the second boy, sir, the one from Project Outcast.'

'Ah yes. Project Outcast.' The president struck a match, held it to the end of his cigar and sucked. The end glowed. 'All dead, eh?' He sucked some more, blowing out clouds of thick smoke. Finally, he cast the match in the ashtray, reclined in his seat and savoured the moment. 'Probably just as well. Can't have those precious genes going astray.'

Mendel nodded. He could feel the president's eyes watching him through the smoke.

'What about bodies?'

Mendel felt himself tense. 'We don't actually have any, sir.'

'None?'

'No, Mr President.'

'Well, how did they die, then?'

'They were shot, sir.'

Puffing hard on his cigar, the president beckoned for more information.

'I had arranged a rendezvous with the boy last night.

He was going to bring me the girl.' Lies wrapped in truth are more easily swallowed. 'We met on the end of the harbour wall in Downtown.'

The president nodded.

'When he arrived, the boy promptly made it clear he had worked out the truth about who he was and where he came from. Presumably through discussion with the girl.'

'Oh.' The president frowned. 'Probably was none too pleased, huh? How the heck did she find out?'

'That I don't know, sir. I'll have to look into it. There's clearly been some kind of security breach on Kravitz's team.'

'Hmm.' The president gestured. 'Go on.'

'The boy, as you rightly said, Mr President, was none too pleased. He quickly became aggressive. When members of my team attempted to restrain him, he produced a gun.' Coughing to clear his throat, Mendel noted the president's small shift forwards in his seat. Hooked on the story? 'The boy and the girl then fled along the harbour wall, sir. Shooting.'

'Your agents, naturally, returned fire?'

Mendel nodded. 'The boy and girl received multiple hits from several heavy-calibre semi-automatic weapons.'

'Must have been ripped to pieces?'

'Yes, sir. They fell from the harbour wall together.'

'And . . .?'

'Sir?'

'No bodies?'

'No, sir. In a matter of seconds they were gone.'

'Gone?' The president's frown deepened.

'Sharks, Mr President. It was a feeding frenzy.'

'Ah! Of course! Now I've gottcha.' The president's gaze drifted for a moment, perhaps contemplating this vicious end. Then he roared with laughter. 'Our darling sharks!' The cigar end glowed. Smoke billowed. 'Well, glad someone's feeding 'em!'

'Yes, sir.'

'So you reckon they both bought it, do you?'

'Yessir, Mr President. No doubt about it. Dead before they hit the water.'

'Excellent!' Suddenly rising to his feet, the president strode over to the window. 'Shame I don't get to raze the damn city. Operation Vengeance really got my blood going. Still . . .' He glanced at Mendel. 'Probably for the best. Don't want to ruffle any feathers in international trade now, do we?'

'No, Mr President.'

'You'll give me a copy of your report?'

'Of course, sir. On your desk by tomorrow morning.'

The president blew a smoke ring. 'Excellent.'

'Thank you, sir.' Mendel bowed his head. 'Will that be all, Mr President?'

The president nodded.

Mendel felt dizzy as he headed for the door.

'Oh, Mendel . . .'

His heart stopped. He turned. The president was scowling. 'Yes, sir?'

'You don't suppose there's a risk any of these precious, special genes of Kravitz's could somehow find their way into . . .' The president trailed off. 'I don't know, I don't understand the science of the thing.' He gesticulated. 'They couldn't somehow, through the food chain . . . with the sharks . . .?'

Mendel smiled and shook his head. 'Rest assured, Mr President. It doesn't work like that.'

'Good.' The president smiled back. 'Didn't think so.'

42

Golden Sand

He was in the wave. One arm extended below like a hydrofoil, lying flat, rigid and straight in the beautifully curving grey-green wall of water. The water was alive, he could feel it bubbling and pulsating around his body as it supported him, carried him, rolled with him, thrust with him, forwards across an endless expanse of ocean.

He turned his head. Riding in the wave beside him, a dolphin. Not just one, but a school of them, playfully leaping and diving in and out of the roaring, rolling water. And in amongst them, was that a mermaid gliding through the surf? She had a young girl's face, hauntingly beautiful, with sparkling green eyes and pale, pale skin. She was smiling. He recognized her . . .

'Phoebe . . .' Kai blinked open his eyes. An azure sky looked down on him. Something wet was lapping at his feet. He lifted his head. The muscles in his neck ached. He was lying on his back on a beach. Ocean at his feet. He looked around. No rocky headland. No harbour. No city. Just golden sand stretching as far as the eye could see in either direction. Sprawled face down, a short distance along the beach, lay a body.

Phoebe. So it hadn't been a dream!

'Phoebe!' As Kai scrambled to his feet he discovered his

neck muscles weren't the only ones to ache. His entire body was stiff. Phoebe's body looked like cold marble. There was no sign of movement.

Gripped by panic, half sprinting, half staggering, he hurried across the soft sand calling Phoebe's name. He dropped to the beach beside her. 'Phoebe?' For a moment he hesitated before putting a hand on her shoulder to shake her. The flesh was warm. Her head moved. The green eyes opened.

'Kai?'

A wave of relief surged through Kai's body. He grinned. 'We made it!'

They had fallen asleep again. Exhausted. The two of them together in each other's arms, on the beach, right where Phoebe lay.

Kai woke first, with Phoebe snuggled against his shoulder. The sun was dropping, and now there were high wisps of cloud in the sky. He felt a deep contentment – body weary but rested. The sand was warm, there was a breeze, and he was happy to lie there still, listening to the ocean and the peaceful sound of Phoebe's breathing.

Something caught his eye. A dot, a speck, a tiny shape moving across the sky, out over the ocean, up towards the clouds. Heavy-lidded still with sleep, he watched. It was too far away to identify, but definitely a bird. Soaring without apparent effort, it slowly drifted closer to land. He watched it now more keenly. Wasn't there something familiar about the form and subtle movements?

Not far from shore, the bird began to turn from its straight course. And as it did so, its underside became illuminated by the sinking sun. Kai shaded his eyes and craned his neck. The bird's shape and its black and white markings were unmistakable. He gasped. His favourite bird!

Phoebe stirred at his side and mumbled.

Kai stroked her head.

Her eyes opened. She smiled. 'You're awake.'

Kai nodded. In the sky, the osprey's turning had taken it full circle. It was going round again.

'What are you watching?' Twisting round on to her back, Phoebe cupped a hand over her eyes.

'An osprey,' said Kai.

'Hey! I saw one of those, out on the headland.'

'They nest there every year.'

'D'you think it's followed us all the way from Dolphins' Point?'

'Maybe,' said Kai.

'And it's watching over us?'

'Maybe. Or it's been here all the time, it's hungry and it's just spotted dinner.'

The osprey hit the water with a flutter of wings and a cry, ascending with its prey.

'Kai?' echoed Phoebe. '*Kai!?* Hey! Did you hear that? The bird just said your name!' Laughing, she threw herself on top of him.

She was strong for her slight frame, and knew how to use her weight. Pushing her off was no simple matter. Kai struggled playfully. 'She swims like a porpoise . . . She interprets birdsong . . .' He smirked. 'Is there no end to this girl's talents?'

Phoebe narrowed her eyes. 'You hear it now?' She grunted, holding him down. 'It's a different cry. You hear that?'

Kai nodded.

'D'you know what it's saying?'

Kai shook his head.

Phoebe grinned. 'It's saying: Kai come back! Kai come back!'

'No!' gasped Kai. 'Please, no!' He laughed. 'Please don't make me . . . this place looks like paradise.' He squeezed her waist. 'And we only just got here!'

PLAYING ON THE EDGE

Neil Arksey

In 2064, major football clubs are so wealthy that no one questions what they are doing to young players. Easy Linker was bought by one of the super-teams when he was thirteen. Now he's escaped with evidence that will destroy them – all he has to do is stay free for long enough . . .

'A thrilling page-turner' – *Sunday Times*

MACB

Neil Arksey

Banksie and MacB have spent all summer working to get into the football team. A fortune teller promises that both will be captain. A load of rubbish – no one plays better than the captain, Duncan King. But then Duncan has a terrible accident. If it is an accident . . .

A highly original reworking of *Macbeth*, this is one of the stories you just can't put down.

hotnews@puffin

Hot off the press!

You'll find all the latest exclusive Puffin news here

Where's it happening?

Check out our author tours and events programme

Bestsellers

What's hot and what's not? Find out in our charts

E-mail updates

Sign up to receive all the latest news
straight to your e-mail box

Links to the coolest sites

Get connected to all the best author web sites

Book of the Month

Check out our recommended reads

www.puffin.co.uk

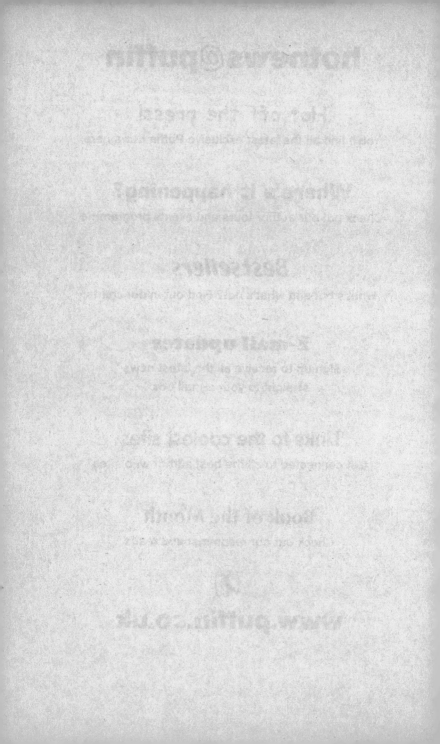